Boy from Berlin

Boy from Berlin

Nancy McDonald

IGUANA

Published by Iguana Books
720 Bathurst Street, Suite 303
Toronto, Ontario, Canada
M5S 2R4

ISBN (paperback): 978-1-77180-264-2
ISBN (hardcover): 978-1-77180-267-3
ISBN (ePub): 978-1-77180-265-9
ISBN (Kindle): 978-1-77180-266-6

Publisher and Editor: Mary Ann J. Blair
Front cover design: Gail Collins and Bern Gorecki
Old toy rabbit: JamieHaxby/iStock.com
Grunge background: Nik Merkulov/Shutterstock.com

This is an original print edition of *Boy from Berlin.*

To Heinz

Who having read this book would have declared,

"I wrote that."

Part One

Berlin, April 1938

Chapter 1

Something was definitely afoot. Most of the servants, including Nanny, had been given the evening off. Just Ursula, the maid, and Marta, our cook, remained on duty. I couldn't remember when that had ever happened. That's why I crept down from the nursery, leaving Peter and Ellen doing their homework. I planned to use my spy skills to find out what was going on.

Mama didn't see me. I hid in the shadows on the landing. But I had a clear view of her through the bannister. I looked through the binoculars Aunt Charlotte had helped me make from two empty toilet paper rolls. Mama stood in the drawing room, smoking a cigarette. As always, she looked elegant. Her curly chestnut hair was swept back from her face and she wore a black fitted dress with a red belt and matching high-heeled shoes. But even from a distance, I could see she was agitated. She paced back and forth across the Turkish carpet. And every few minutes she looked at her wristwatch, the gold one Father had made her himself, a gift for their first wedding anniversary.

The doorbell rang. It was so loud, I almost jumped. I shrank back deeper into the dark and watched Ursula cross the front hall, her shoes clicking on the shiny parquet floor. Ursula was new. She always did as Mama asked, but her attitude was faintly superior. Almost as if she was better than Mama.

As she opened the front door, cool air rushed in. It had that sharp, fresh smell that promised rain.

"Good evening, Fräulein Charlotte." She greeted my aunt pleasantly enough then self-consciously patted her thin blonde hair, which was tidily braided in coils and pinned securely.

Aunt Charlotte! Mama hadn't mentioned she was coming. Maybe we could play hide and seek after she and Mama visited. Like we'd done on Saturday. I adored my aunt. We all did. Mama called her a maverick. I wasn't exactly sure what that meant, but she didn't particularly care what other people thought of her. And she was the only woman I knew who regularly wore trousers. Tonight she must have come directly from work, though, because she had on a severe grey suit. She looked serious.

"Good evening, Ursula." Aunt Charlotte had a throaty voice that commanded attention.

Ursula stood a bit straighter. "Frau Avigdor has been waiting for you."

At the sound of the doorbell, Mama had put out her cigarette and come to the drawing-room doorway. She hugged Aunt Charlotte and kissed her on both cheeks.

She turned to Ursula. "Thank you. You may have the rest of the evening off, and tell Cook she can go too, as soon as she's laid out dinner."

"Very good, Madame. I'll be back at eleven o'clock."

Ursula turned, smiled slyly, and disappeared with Aunt Charlotte's coat and hat. Mama and my aunt walked arm in arm into the drawing room. Mama slid the door firmly closed behind them.

Now what? I wouldn't be able to hear what they were saying from where I was hiding. But with the servants out, Father still at work, and Peter and Ellen safely on the third floor, I decided to risk eavesdropping. I crept down the stairs, careful to avoid the few creaky spots, and crouched down silently, my ear pressed against the door.

I was in luck. They talked quietly, but by concentrating hard, I could just make out their words.

"Else, I've had a long day and I'm tired. What's so important you couldn't tell me over the telephone?"

"We're leaving tonight, Lotte. Rifat says we can't wait any longer."

4

My heart started to pound. I hoped Mama and Aunt Charlotte wouldn't hear it.

"Tonight! Do the children know?"

"No, we didn't want them to say anything to their friends. Once Rifat gets home, we'll have dinner and tell them. We'll pack up a few things and be gone before the servants get back." Mama paused. "Lotte, for the last time, will you come with us?"

Aunt Charlotte sighed. "We've been through this, Else. I can't leave Berlin now. My work is too important. Even if I could, where would I get a job? Where would I live?"

"You know you can stay with our friends until you find something. It isn't safe here anymore, Lotte. We've already lost our citizenship and Rifat thinks it won't be long before we lose the house and everything in it. And for you it's even more dangerous."

I frowned. What was so dangerous about working as a secretary in an automobile factory?

"Why tonight, Else?"

Silence. Then Mama, her voice lowered, said, "Yesterday, Peter had a new teacher, a Herr Vogel. He wore a Nazi Party uniform. He made Peter's friend—you know him, Miriam Hirsch's son Solly—stand at the front of the room while he pointed out how he was 'different' because he was Jewish."

My aunt gasped.

"How long before that happens to Peter? Or Ellen? Or little Heinz?" I heard the catch in Mama's voice. "And now that Peter is ten it would draw attention if he didn't join the *Deutsches Jungvolk*. We can't stay in Germany." What did Mama mean? Peter couldn't wait to be part of the German Youth and go hiking and camping with the older boys.

Mama paused, and when she spoke again it was in her most persuasive voice. "Berlin has changed, Lotte. You know this. Nazi soldiers strutting in the streets. Hitler Youth swearing allegiance to that man. More restrictions for Jews every week."

5

More silence as my aunt absorbed this.

"But your friends, Else, they're taking in the five of you already," said Aunt Charlotte slowly. "They won't want a sixth. Don't worry. I'll be all right here until you're settled in your own home. Then, I promise, I'll join you."

"You must, Lotte. Your life depends on it. I can't live without you and neither can the children. You know how they treasure you."

At that, both Mama and my aunt choked back sobs. The grandfather clock struck just as a motor car turned into the drive. Father was home! I scurried back up the stairs to the third floor, my mind in a whirl.

The nursery was my favourite room in the house. It was cozy with its light green walls and multicoloured quilts. The lamps on all three bedside tables gave the room a warm glow. Outside, the setting sun streaked the clouds pink. New leaves covered the linden tree just outside the front window and the soft cooing of a rock dove floated through the open window.

Peter lay on his stomach in bed, reading. Ellen—or Bibi as we mostly called her—was crouched at her dollhouse, putting up the miniature framed portrait of Adolf Hitler that her friend Anneliese had given her that afternoon. When she'd seen it, Mama had pursed her lips and turned away without a word. There were posters of Hitler all over Berlin. He promised to save Germany, but Mama and Father didn't like him at all.

"Are we Jewish?" I blurted out.

Peter looked up and rolled his dark eyes. "Of course not," he said in that superior tone he often used with me. "What would make you think that?"

"Mama just told Aunt Charlotte that we're leaving Berlin—"

"Leaving Berlin?" Bibi interrupted. "Why?"

"I don't know. But I think it has something to do with being Jewish."

"Did Mama say we're Jewish?" Peter closed his book with a snap and sat up. He swung his legs around, put his feet on the floor, and stared at me.

"Not exactly, but—"

"You're sure you heard Mama say we're leaving?" Bibi interrupted again.

"Yes, tonight—"

"We can't just leave tonight," Peter cut me off. "My science fair is in two weeks. Papa said he would come. I know he'll be impressed with the microscope I made using fuse wire and water. It's *ingenious*." Peter was a year older than Bibi and two years older than me. He liked to use big words we didn't understand.

Bibi suddenly remembered her upcoming art show. "You must have heard wrong, Käfer," she said, using the nickname Mama had given me because I'd been born on May 1, when the *Maikäfers*— May bugs—appeared. "Mama and Papa have to see my painting of the Elephant Gate at the Zoo. Herr Weber says my brushwork has really improved."

"Mama said we were leaving," I insisted. "And she talked about Jews—"

"We're not Jewish," Peter said definitely. "I think Papa and Mama would have told us if we were. Besides, we don't go to a Jewish school or to church on Saturday."

"But—"

Bibi suddenly put her fingers to her lips. "Hush," she said. We heard Mama's footsteps coming up the stairs.

"Don't let on I told you anything," I begged them.

"Maybe you should stop being a snoop," Peter said in a loud whisper.

"I'm not a snoop," I shot back indignantly. "I'm a spy."

"Not a very good one."

7

"Better than you."

Mama poked her head inside the door. "What are you three talking about?" Her voice sounded unnaturally cheerful to me. She didn't wait for an answer. "Papa is home and it's time for dinner. Come."

We looked at each other and instantly formed a silent pact. Neither of them would give me away. We followed Mama wordlessly down the stairs.

There was no sign of Aunt Charlotte or Father, but the dining room table was set and Marta had left cold cuts and salad on the sideboard.

"You sit down, Käfer. I'll make you a plate." Mama tousled my hair.

Then, suddenly, Father was there. Wearing his trademark navy suit. He wasn't particularly tall, but he filled the room. Mama's friends declared him dashing and clustered around him at parties, hanging on his every word. I tried not to attract too much of his attention. Ever. I always seemed to annoy him. I looked at my plate as Mama put it down in front of me.

Father stroked his sleek, dark moustache as he surveyed us quickly. He was very proud of the hair on his upper lip.

"You're all very quiet." He helped himself to some food then took his place at the head of the table. "Is there something I should know?"

He didn't wait for us to answer. "Your Mother and I have something to tell you." He looked at Mama. "We're going away tonight. All of us. To The Hague."

"The Hague? In Holland?" said Peter, doing a good impression of someone who hadn't already heard the news we were leaving Berlin. Perhaps he really hadn't believed me.

"On a holiday, Papa?" Peter continued.

"Not a holiday. I've been offered a better job."

"We're moving?" Peter asked, brushing back a forelock that always fell into his eyes.

"Yes."

"But what about school? And our friends?" Bibi wanted to know.

"You'll go to a new school, and you'll make new friends, Schatzi. You're good at it," Papa smiled. But Bibi, her brow furrowed, didn't notice. She was probably thinking about her two best friends, Anneliese and Erika. They were all "blood sisters," she'd told me. They'd pricked their fingers until they drew blood, then rubbed them together.

"But my science fair—"

"We'll miss that, Peter. And Bibi's art show. I'm sorry."

Into the silence that followed I looked at Mama and blurted out, "Do we have to leave because we're Jewish?"

Mama's mouth dropped slightly, but she quickly closed it.

Father turned to me. His voice was tight. "What is the matter with you, Heinz? I told you. I have a new job. That's it. No more questions. Any of you." His steely gaze moved from me to Bibi to Peter. "Eat your dinner. Then Mama will help you pack. We've got a long journey ahead of us and I want to leave by ten o'clock."

I ducked my head and shrank down in my seat. But the servants wouldn't be back until later! No goodbye to Nanny, who always had a special hug for me. Or Marta with her treats when I came in from the park. Or Fritz, who let me wear his cap and sit behind the steering wheel while I pretended to drive Father's motor car.

Mama reached over and squeezed my hand. I looked at her and she gave me a little smile. But I wasn't consoled. I'd seen the look in her eyes when I'd said the word *Jewish*.

After dinner, we helped Mama drag the suitcases out from the back of the cupboard. I hadn't used mine since I'd gone to Rome with her and Father over a year ago. It looked a lot smaller than I remembered.

"How am I going to fit all my things in there?"

Bibi and Peter were staring at their suitcases, and I knew they were thinking the same thing.

"We're not taking everything now," explained Mama. "We're packing as if we're going on a holiday. It's spring in The Hague, so take some of your lighter clothes."

"What about our toys and books?" asked Bibi.

"Just take one of each. Your favourites."

"But, Mama—"

"Don't argue, Bibi." Mama sighed. "I'll get Ursula to send us the rest once we're settled. Come now, let's get going."

I didn't much care what clothes Mama chose, but I wasn't going anywhere without Funny Bunny Blue! Aunt Charlotte had brought him back from England when I was born. His real name was Peter Rabbit, but I called him Funny Bunny Blue because of his blue coat. He slept with me every night even though Peter said eight was much too old to be cuddling a stuffed animal.

I grabbed him from under my pillow. Mama smiled. A real smile. "Of course you can take your bunny, Käfer," she said. "Now, let's see what else you'll need. Then I'll help you and Peter, Bibi."

We spent the next few hours debating what to take and what to leave behind. I felt like I was in a dream.

Then Father called from the landing downstairs. "Are you nearly done? We need to leave now."

"We're coming, Rifat," Mama called back. She closed the top of my suitcase and snapped the two brass clasps shut. "Peter, you can take your own bag. Bibi, I'll carry yours and Käfer's."

"Käfer, your book!" said Bibi.

I ran back to my bedside table and picked up *Emil and the Detectives*. Nanny and I had been reading it together. How would I find out if Emil got his money back from the mysterious Herr

Grundeis? Emil was smart and brave. I longed to be like him. Then I knew Father would notice me. In a good way.

Father was waiting for us in the front hall. On the round, marble-topped table, beside a vase filled with tall pink cherry boughs, was a little pile of white envelopes. The top one had *Nanny* written on it in Father's large, neat script. Gifts for the servants. Like Father gave them at Christmas.

Mama glanced at them, then at Father. They exchanged a look filled with private thoughts.

"Here, let me take that," Father said, reaching for my suitcase. "All ready?"

Chapter 2

As we walked out to the motor car, our feet crunching on the gravel drive, the rain fell softly. Father told Bibi to sit between me and Peter in the back seat. I silently thanked him.

Father knew how to drive even though Fritz took him to and from work every day. Before he met Mama, Father had been an amateur sports car racer. He loved to visit automobile factories. One of his good friends was Ferdinand Porsche, the famous German motor car maker.

When we were all settled, breathing in the scent of polished leather, he started the engine. "We're off." His voice sounded falsely bright.

As we pulled out of the drive, Fritz's bald head appeared suddenly in the window above the garage, illuminated by the headlights. His mouth dropped open. Then, as we started down the street, Ursula appeared, walking toward the house. When she saw the motor car, she ran quickly through the gate and up the back walk. Why was she in such a hurry? Then I forgot all about her as I watched our house disappear.

No one spoke as we glided through the quiet streets. There were few people about, even on the larger avenues. I'd never been out in the city this late, but I'd always imagined it was busy like it was during the day. Father and Mama went to restaurants and cabarets at night with friends and talked about how exciting the city was. Though now that I thought about it, they hadn't done that in a long time.

Other things had changed, too.

In the last several months some of Mama's prized paintings had disappeared, including her cherished *Portrait of a Young Woman*, done by an artist called Botticelli. The frame had left marks on the wall so Otto, the gardener, had touched up the paint. He put up another painting, but Mama looked sad every time she looked at it.

Then, last week, I'd gone looking for Mama and found her sewing in her room. Before she saw me, she slipped an emerald necklace into the lining of one of her dresses. Then she looked up and gazed at me silently for a moment. She calmly asked me what I wanted and went back to her sewing. As if she stitched gems into her clothes every day.

And now, tonight, we were leaving in the dark without saying goodbye to anyone. Not even Aunt Charlotte. Why hadn't she stayed until we'd left? I couldn't even ask Mama because I wasn't supposed to know about Aunt Charlotte's visit.

A loud clap of thunder overhead was followed by a flash of lightning. The rain fell faster, drumming on the roof of the motor car. The red Nazi banners that flew from virtually every building along the boulevard began to droop. Father turned a corner and, suddenly, just ahead of us was a large crowd. The people were shouting and raising their fists in front of a shop on the right. I couldn't make out what they were saying, just that they were angry. I felt Bibi tense beside me. She took my hand. It was moist.

"Damn," Father said under his breath.

"Can't we turn around?" said Mama. Her voice was higher than usual.

"Not now," said Father tersely. That's when I saw the soldier on a motorcycle drive towards us. "Stay quiet. I'll do the talking."

Father rolled down the window. The soldier wore shiny black boots that came to his knees and the belt around his waist had a pistol holder. Rain dripped from his peaked cap.

"Good evening, sergeant," Father said before the soldier could speak. "My wife and three young children are with me and I'm worried for their safety. Can you get us away from here before it turns violent?" It was not quite an order.

"Where are you headed this late at night, sir?" asked the sergeant. He ran his flashlight over us quickly. I blinked at the brightness of it.

"To The Hague. We have a family funeral to attend. We couldn't leave any earlier, as I was pressed at work today." Father reached into his breast pocket and handed the soldier his business card. We all held our breath as he peered closely at it. Apparently satisfied, he handed it back with a salute, his right arm out straight. "*Sieg Heil*. Important work. Follow me, Herr Avigdor. I'll get you out of here now."

The sergeant got back on his motorcycle, revved the engine, and did a U-turn in the now wet street. He signalled to Father to do the same. As we turned, I saw the crowd clearly in the light from the street lamps. Their shouts grew louder. Some of them were painting the word *Jude*—Jew—on the building, oblivious to the rain, their faces contorted with rage. As more people ran to join them, one man threw a brick through the shop window. At the sound of breaking glass, the crowd roared approval. Behind them several soldiers on motorcycles laughed as they watched. I shivered.

We followed the sergeant for a few blocks. He pulled over. Father followed suit.

"You should be fine now, sir. This road will take you toward The Hague. Safe travels." Again, he gave Father that salute, then drove off in the direction we had come from.

Mama sighed loudly. "Oh, Rifat," was all she said.

He reached over and patted her arm. "It's all right, Else."

We were all quiet as Father drove out of the city. I was frightened and confused. Why hadn't the soldiers stepped in to stop the angry crowd? Why had they just looked on and laughed?

It reminded me of something that happened two weeks earlier. I had forgotten about it, but the memory rushed back now.

Mama picked me up from school. It was an unusually warm spring day. Big puffy white clouds dotted the blue sky. The cherry trees were covered in brilliant pink blossoms. And everyone in Berlin seemed to be outside, smiles on their faces, after the long winter.

Mama was in high spirits. "Let's stop at Herr Meier's on the way home, Käfer," she said in her musical voice. Mama had trained to be an opera singer, but then she met Father at a soirée at a friend's house and it was "love at first sight."

When we got to the café, Herr Meier rushed over and gave Mama a little bow. I noticed Mama had that effect on most men. "Pleased to see you, Frau Avigdor. And you, young master Heinz. You are grown taller, yes? Please to sit here and enjoy the sun." Herr Meier was from Belgium and often muddled the order of his words. He held Mama's chair for her. "What you would like?" He looked at me.

"*Himbeersaft, bitte*," I said. Herr Meier's raspberry juice was one of my favourite treats.

"*Eiskaffee* for me," replied Mama with a smile.

As Herr Meier bustled off to get our order, Mama gave me her full attention. "What was the most interesting thing you learned at school today?"

"That's easy, Mama. About the Egyptians." Herr Wagner had told us how the pharaohs had enslaved the Jews, but I knew Mama wouldn't want to hear about that. "Did you know it took thousands of people twenty years or more to build just one pyramid? And that the pharaohs took everything they needed for their afterlife into the pyramid with them—even their pets! Can we get a dog—"

"Perhaps you will be an archaeologist one day." Mama didn't want an animal in the house.

"What's an archaeologist?"

15

"Someone who studies things people leave behind to understand how they lived. That's how we know about the pharaohs."

I thought about it. "Maybe, Mama. I know I want to see the pyramids one day. And go in a boat down the Nile and—"

"*What* is going on?" Mama interrupted.

Young voices, growing louder, came from around the corner.

She looked over her shoulder in the direction of the noise.

"I'll find out," I offered.

Five of Peter's classmates crowded together in the street. I recognized them. Four of them had encircled Eli Nussbaum. Eli was short and pudgy and bit his nails to the quick. But he was good-natured. I liked him. He always had a smile for me. He was practically blind without his glasses, and they were being held high in the air in the hand of one of his tormentors.

"Give them back, Kurt," Eli begged. His bottom lip quivered. His dark brown eyes teared up. "You know I can't see without them."

"You going to cry now?" taunted one of the others, as Eli choked back a sob.

"Why aren't you wearing a skullcap?" another one goaded. "You pretending you're not a Jew?"

"Think we wouldn't know anyway?" chimed in the third.

Eli was silent, but his whole body trembled.

I wanted to do something to make them stop. But I was dumbstruck.

"You want your glasses back?" asked Kurt, his face twisted with fury. He leaned forward and yelled right in Eli's face. "Jump for them, *Judenschwein*."

"Yes, jump for them *du dicker Jude*," the others cried, moving closer to him. One of the boys poked Eli in the stomach with his finger. They all laughed as tears ran down Eli's face.

"Jump! If you can reach them, I'll give them back to you," Kurt taunted. "Then again, maybe I won't. Maybe I'll smash them—"

My mouth formed the word "stop," but nothing came out.

"You will give them back right this instant," Mama thundered. I hadn't noticed she had come up behind me. I barely recognized her voice. I'd never heard her so angry.

"I don't—" Kurt started to say nastily, but when he saw Mama, he gulped nervously. She wasn't a tall woman, but at that moment she was formidable. Kurt seemed to shrink on the spot.

"And you will apologize to Eli."

"But he's a—" one started to protest.

Mama stared him down. "All of you. Now."

"Sorry," they said sullenly as Kurt returned Eli's glasses.

"Now go home. You must have homework to do." As the four boys slunk off up the street, Kurt muttered, "Jew lover."

He didn't intend for Mama to hear and she didn't. She was handing Eli her handkerchief. "Wipe your tears and blow your nose," she said kindly. "Heinz and I will walk you home."

I spied Herr Meier peeking around the corner to see what the commotion was about, but Mama had forgotten all about our treat and I didn't feel like it anymore. Not even *Himbeersaft*.

Later, after we saw Eli home and went back to pay Herr Meier, Mama said, "Those boys deserve a good thrashing, although they're unlikely to get it from their fathers. It's never acceptable to bully anyone, Käfer. Not for the way they look—or for the religion they practise. No matter what Herr Hitler says." She spoke the last words softly, almost to herself.

Poor Eli. It must be hard to be different.

I replayed the scene in my mind. Kurt and the others had picked on Eli because he was Jewish. But is that why Mama had reacted so fiercely? Or was she angry because they took his glasses and made him cry?

Eventually, the steady sound of the rain hitting the motor car roof lulled me to sleep. I woke up when it started to become light. It had stopped raining, though there were still some dark clouds tinged with pink in the sky. In the front seat Father and Mama talked quietly.

"We need to stop soon, Rifat. Is the *Gasthaus* close? The children will be hungry and we all need to clean up and use the toilet."

"It's in the next village. Bernhard assured me we can get breakfast there." Bernhard, or Herr Berkovitch as I called him, was Father's business partner and good friend.

"And if anyone asks where we're going?"

"We tell them what I told the sergeant. Best to stick as close as possible to the same story."

I knew Bibi was awake now too and probably Peter as well, but we just sat quietly. The countryside was beautiful. Lush green meadows, dotted with trees coming into bud. In the distance was a hill and atop it sat the ruins of a castle.

Other than the trip to Rome with Father and Mama, I hadn't been outside Berlin before. I'd been to the park across from our house with Nanny, and Mama often took us to the Tiergarten and the Zoo, but this was very different. It was exciting. I felt butterflies in my stomach as I thought about The Hague. What would our new life be like?

"Here's the village," said Father. "And there is the *Gasthaus*, just as Bernhard said, on the right."

We pulled to a stop beside an old house with white stucco walls, criss-crossed in spots by wood beams. There were colourful flower boxes at every window. A sign above the door read *Klein Gasthaus*. At that moment, the door opened and a short, stout woman appeared. Her face was flushed and a few grey hairs had escaped her bun, but her smile was welcoming.

18

"I thought I heard a motor car! Have you been driving long?" she said to Father and Mama as they emerged. She wiped her hands lightly on her apron. Then she saw Peter, Bibi and me climb out of the back seat, rubbing the sleep from our eyes. "Oh, lovely children! You must be hungry. Come inside. I'm just getting breakfast on the table now. You can clean up and join my other guests. I'm Frau Klein."

She led us into the inn. "Where have you come from?" she asked Mama in a singsong voice.

"Berlin."

"That's a long drive." She pointed to the hallway on our left. "Toilets are down there, one for ladies and one for men. I must get back to my other guests. Come along when you're ready."

Father, Peter and I went into the men's toilet. Father checked to be sure there was no one else there, then turned to us. He crouched down and spoke softly. "If anyone asks you where we're going, you tell them it's to a family funeral. Your mother's aunt just died in The Hague. Understand?"

"Yes, Papa," said Peter.

Father looked hard at me. I nodded.

"Now use the toilet and wash your face," he said.

I did as I was told. Then, after Father had passed his comb through my hair with no noticeable improvement—it was curly like Mama's—I went into the hall to wait. I was looking at the pictures on the wall when a stranger came walking down the corridor toward me. He wore a uniform similar to the one the soldier had worn the night before and those same, shiny black boots. He carried a two-tone visor cap with white piping in his right hand. On his upper left arm was a red armband with a swastika on it. A wave of cigarette smoke accompanied him.

I tensed.

"Hello, young man." He was pleasant enough, but I remembered the other soldier and how Father and Mama had reacted to him.

"Hello, sir." My voice was hardly more than a whisper.

"I haven't seen you before."

"No, sir. We just arrived."

"Ah, you came in the Maybach Zeppelin parked outside." He arched one eyebrow. "That's a beautiful motor car."

I just nodded.

"Where have you driven from?"

"Berlin." Why was he asking so many questions?

"That's a long way. And where are you going?"

"The Hague."

The door to the men's toilet opened and Father appeared, Peter right behind. Father looked at me and then at the stranger.

"Heinz. Are you behaving?" He spoke sharply, but his eyes were kind, so I knew he wasn't angry with me.

"He's being perfectly charming, sir," the stranger answered for me. "He was just telling me you are the owner of that fine motor car."

"I am indeed. My business is aeroplanes, but I must confess, I love motor cars." Father smiled and stroked his moustache. Even after driving through the night, he looked immaculate in his tailor-made navy blue suit, crisp white shirt, and shiny leather shoes. "Rifat Avigdor. Director of Deutsche Benzinuhren-Gesellschaft." Just as he had the night before, Father handed the soldier his business card.

He looked down at it, then back at Father. He smiled, but it didn't reach his eyes. "Rifat Avigdor. That's not a German name."

"It's Turkish," answered Papa. "I was born in Constantinople. I came to Germany many years ago to study aeronautical engineering and stayed. This is my elder son, Peter, and Heinz you've met." As Mama and Bibi emerged from the ladies toilet, Father turned. "My wife Else and daughter Ellen."

"Captain Rolf König, at your service." He clicked his heels and held out his hand to Mama, who took it briefly. The smile he gave her seemed genuine.

20

"A pleasure." Mama turned to Father. She, too, looked remarkably fresh despite hours sitting in the motor car. Mama was always chic. That was the word Aunt Charlotte used. "Rifat, the children are famished and so am I. Shall we go in to breakfast?"

Mama led the way to the dining room; the captain, still inquisitive, followed with Father.

"You are on your way to The Hague, your son Heinz tells me."

"Yes, my wife's favourite aunt died suddenly. We didn't want to miss the funeral."

"Your wife is Dutch?"

"German, but her aunt married a Dutch man." Father lied so convincingly, I was beginning to believe Mama really had an aunt in The Hague.

"Ah, I wondered at you taking the children away so close to the end of the school year."

"They're excellent students and we won't be gone long."

Father picked up his step. We reached the dining room. Frau Klein pointed us to our table. The captain nodded and joined a pretty young woman at a table across from us. Her blonde hair fell in curls to her shoulders, framing her wide-set eyes, pert nose, and bright red lips. In her tight blue dress, she seemed out of place in the *Gasthaus* somehow. When she saw me look over at her, she smiled and winked. I smiled back shyly, then quickly turned away. She laughed merrily.

There were cold cuts, sausages, cheeses, and fresh bread, but my stomach was clenched in a knot. I picked at my food, even though Mama encouraged me to eat. We didn't talk much. From time to time, the captain looked over at us. The expression on his face was hard to read. He seemed nice enough on the surface, but there was a watchfulness about him. As if he was trying to decide something.

When we were finished, Father asked Frau Klein for the bill. As he paid, the captain got up from his table and came over.

21

He held out his hand to Mama again. "I am sorry for your loss," he said.

"Thank you. I will miss my aunt terribly."

"Unfortunately, I am travelling to Berlin, or I would give you an escort to the border as your husband is such an important man to the German aircraft industry." This was directed at Father.

"Too bad," said Father smoothly. "Safe travels, captain. Thank you, Frau Klein, for a most enjoyable breakfast. We shall stop again here in a few days on our way back to Berlin."

Peter, Bibi, and I ran quickly to the toilet then went outside to join Father and Mama. They were leaning against the motor car, talking quietly. We were just about to climb in to the back seat when Frau Klein bustled out with a large wicker basket in her hand. A black-and-white cat trotted behind her.

As I bent down to stroke him, she said loudly, "I packed some food for you. I noticed the little one didn't eat too much. He'll be hungry again soon."

"Thank you. That's very kind," said Mama.

As Father reached for the basket, Frau Klein, her back turned to the *Gasthaus*, lowered her voice. She spoke quickly.

"The captain is very interested in you, Herr Avigdor. He wrote down your vehicle registration number and asked to use the phone. I heard him calling Gestapo headquarters in Berlin. They're not people whose attention you want to attract. Be careful, sir."

Chapter 3

Peter, Bibi, and I looked at one another. What was the Gestapo? Frau Klein made it sound like something to be feared. And Father and Mama's reactions confirmed it. Their faces drained of colour completely.

"In the motor car. Quickly—" Father said. He handed Frau Klein some bills. She protested, but he insisted. Then he helped Mama into the front seat.

"I thought showing him my card would deflect his attention," he said to her. "But it seems to have done just the opposite." Clearly, Father was angry with himself.

When he got in behind the wheel, he turned to us. His voice was serious. "We may be stopped by the military before we reach the border with Holland. I need you to do as I say quickly and without arguing. Understood?"

We all nodded. Nothing had really happened, but I had never been more frightened in my life.

The sights outside the window no longer entertained me. All I could think about was what would happen to us if we were caught by the Gestapo. I couldn't even imagine. But it was clear it would be bad. Who were they and why would they want to hurt us? What had we done wrong?

Bibi wiggled in her seat and pulled out *Emil and the Detectives,* which had slipped behind her and was poking into her back. She handed it to me. What would Emil do if he met the Gestapo?

We drove for a long time, passing the occasional motor car or truck, mostly going the other direction.

Father spoke reassuringly. "It won't be long now until we reach the border and we're into Holland."

I settled into my seat and let out a deep breath. Everything was going to be all right. The Gestapo, whoever they were, weren't going to hurt us.

"Rifat." There was a tremor in Mama's voice. She was looking in the side mirror. Father's eyes went to the rear-view mirror. His face went pale all over again. I turned. A black motor car was coming up quickly behind us.

Father kept driving at the same speed, but then the motor car surged ahead in the other lane. The soldier in the passenger seat signalled him to stop. Father pulled over and the soldiers climbed out of their motor car.

This time, there were two of them. One tall. The other was average height. He had dark circles under his eyes and smothered a yawn. They both gave the *Heil* salute. The tall one, a lieutenant, looked displeased when Father didn't return it.

"You don't salute the Führer?" he asked.

"It's hard to salute sitting behind the wheel of a motor car," Father said mildly. "We are in a hurry, lieutenant. My wife's aunt has died in The Hague and we have a funeral to get to."

Taking charge didn't work this time.

"I need to see your papers." The lieutenant was curt.

"They're in my suitcase in the boot," said Father. He got out of the motor car. The lieutenant followed him. The other soldier stayed where he was. He didn't pull out his gun, but I didn't like the way he stared at us.

I turned in my seat and watched as Father retrieved our passports from his bag and handed them to the lieutenant, who opened the first one. He frowned and spoke sharply to Father.

"You are in charge of one of the country's largest aeroplane parts companies and you are not a German citizen? You are a clever man, I hear. I'm not sure you should be leaving the country, particularly in the company of your family. For all I know, you are not coming back and you may be taking secrets with you."

How did he know what Father did for a living? Father hadn't mentioned it. It must have been that soldier at the *Gasthaus*! Frau Klein had been right.

Father needed help. I didn't stop to think. I opened the door and ran to him. I blurted out the first thing that came into my head. "Pardon me, Papa, but can I have Funny Bunny Blue?"

Father's eyes widened in disbelief, but before he could answer, the lieutenant put his hand on my shoulder.

"Who is Funny Bunny Blue?" he asked, not unkindly. He was younger than Father and had piercing blue eyes, pale skin, and a close-cropped blonde moustache.

"He's my bunny rabbit," I said, forcing my voice not to tremble. "I've had him since I was born. My Aunt Charlotte gave him to me."

"Is it Aunt Charlotte who has died?"

"No, it's my other aunt. Luna." I could lie as convincingly as Papa. Luna was Papa's sister who lived in Rome. And was very much alive.

The lieutenant dropped down on one knee so that his face was almost level with mine. "Ah, so Funny Bunny Blue is your special friend."

I nodded. "My brother says I'm too old for him, but I don't think so. I tell Funny Bunny Blue everything."

"And you couldn't leave him behind in Berlin for even a few days?"

"Oh, no, sir. I take him everywhere with me."

The lieutenant gazed at me for a long moment. I didn't blink. "I have a son about the same age as you. He's in Dresden with his *Mutter* and I haven't seen him in weeks. But I'm sure he still takes his Steiff bear to bed with him every night. What's your name?"

"Heinz," I replied.

"Good German name. My boy is called Dieter. You remind me of him." He stood up and patted me on the head. "Heinz should have his rabbit," he said to Father.

As Father reached for my suitcase, the lieutenant watched him, then looked back at me, deep in thought. When Father handed me Funny Bunny Blue, I hugged him close and gave the lieutenant my most winning smile. The one Mama could never resist.

For just an instant, his face softened. If I hadn't been looking right at him, I wouldn't have caught it.

He raised his voice so that the other soldier, who was still watching Mama, Peter, and Bibi, could hear.

"Open the suitcases, Herr Avigdor," he ordered. "I want to take a look."

Father did as he was told. As the lieutenant rifled through them, the motor car's boot shielding his voice from the other soldier, he spoke quietly and quickly. "Your name is on a Gestapo list of people to watch. Should you try to leave the country, you will be turned back at border control and quite possibly imprisoned or sent to a detention camp."

As he closed the boot, he called to the other soldier. "His story checks out. Just clothes and personal items. Enough for a few days."

He turned back to Father. "Go now." He gave me a small smile. "Keep Funny Bunny Blue safe, Heinz."

Then he walked back toward his motor car.

"You're letting them go?" the other soldier asked, falling into step with him. He sounded a bit surprised, but he didn't argue. He yawned loudly.

"You should drink less beer at night," said the lieutenant. "We've got no reason to apprehend them. There is nothing related to his work in his suitcase or in the boot. Let border control do its job."

"And if they avoid border control and try to leave by crossing the fields?"

"They'll have to be very lucky to avoid the armed patrols."

The tired soldier shrugged his shoulders. They both got in their motor car, did a U-turn, and drove off in the direction they had come from.

When they were out of sight, Father looked at me and asked, "What made you do that?"

"I thought about Emil."

He cocked one eyebrow.

"You know. *Emil and the Detectives*. How Emil helps his mother by being clever and brave."

Father looked at me. Really looked at me. As if he was seeing me for the first time.

"You were both, Käfer." He used Mama's pet name for me.

My heart swelled with happiness.

Chapter 4

"Crossing at border control is not possible," Papa announced when he got back into the motor car. "We'll have to walk through these fields tonight. While we wait for it to turn dark, we'll sightsee and have a picnic. How fortunate Frau Klein packed us a basket."

We drove along back roads for hours. From time to time, Mama pointed things out to us—a white stork flying past, cows grazing peacefully, an abandoned barn—but I was thinking about what we would be doing later. Crossing a farmer's fields in the dark, dodging military patrols. I shivered with apprehension. I longed to be at home in the nursery, Nanny tucking me in and reading to me from *Emil and the Detectives*. Did Nanny miss me? I wondered.

We stopped eventually and Papa helped Mama spread a blanket down on the ground. We opened Frau Klein's basket. It was full to the brim with sausages, hard boiled eggs, assorted cheeses, and a fresh loaf of bread. There was even a bottle of homemade wine for Papa and Mama.

"It all looks quite delicious," Mama said, clapping her hands together. "Eat up. We have a lot of walking to do later."

I found I was hungry. We all were. The food cheered us up, and we even managed to talk and laugh while we ate.

"Papa, why did that sergeant say you weren't German?" Peter asked suddenly. "We're German, aren't we? We were born here."

Papa paused. He was clearly thinking about what to say. "We are in our hearts, Peter," he said finally.

Peter and Bibi looked as confused as I was.

"You'd better explain, Rifat," Mama said.

Father took a deep breath. "Hitler has taken away the citizenship of many Germans, including all of us," he said slowly. "That means we don't have German passports and the German government won't protect us."

"But how can he do that?" I asked, emboldened by the glow of Papa's approval.

"He passed a law."

"But why, Papa?"

"Because there are many people Hitler doesn't like and we're among them."

"Why doesn't he like us?" I wanted to know.

Papa and Mama exchanged a look. "Because we don't agree with him and what he's doing to Germany. Enough now. Let's get going."

I wanted to ask if we weren't German, what were we, but Papa was done explaining.

Mama smiled at me as she packed up the basket. "That was quick thinking this morning, Käfer. And brave, too." Bibi agreed, hugging me. Even Peter looked at me with grudging approval.

"He reminds me of Lotte sometimes," Papa said. "Fearless and impetuous."

A shadow came over Mama's face. Papa looked sorry he'd reminded Mama of Aunt Charlotte.

"It worked out well this time, Käfer, but from now on, do as I say," he said. He put his hand on my cheek. It was warm. It felt good.

We drove back to where the soldiers had stopped us hours earlier. Papa surveyed the field and drove further down the road, closer to the border. The sun was setting. It would be dark soon.

"We'll leave the motor car here," he said. He reached into the glove box and removed a flashlight. "That stand of trees over there will give us some protection from prying eyes. Stay inside until I tell you to come out."

Papa went around to the back of the motor car, bent down and started to let the air out of the tire on the passenger side. Then he got out the mother of pearl pocket knife he always carried and punctured the tire several times. It didn't take long for it to go flat.

He called to us and we joined him.

"Anyone going past will think we've gone for help," he explained. He picked up his and Mama's suitcases. Peter took his own and Mama carried Bibi's and mine. I held Funny Bunny Blue tightly under my arm. We set off across the field.

By the time we reached the stand of trees it was nearly dark. It took longer than Papa thought it would, partly because it was harder to walk on newly turned soil than it was on pavement, but also because every time we heard a vehicle on the road, we lay down flat on the ground to avoid being seen.

"Rifat, we need a break," said Mama, dropping the suitcases. Even in the dim light I could see that her face was flushed and streaked with dust. "How much further is it, do you think?"

"At least twice as far as we've already walked." Papa looked uncharacteristically rumpled too.

Mama removed her high-heeled shoes and handed them to me. "Please carry these for me Käfer. It will be easier to walk without them."

Papa looked at us. "We can do it. We must."

We sat in the woods for a while, waiting for the sun to go down completely. When it did, it was really dark. The only light came from the crescent moon and the stars. Then I spotted a tiny light ahead of us in the distance.

"Papa, look."

I thought he'd be happy at the thought of people, but he cautioned, "We must be very quiet. It's hard to know who is friend and who is foe these days. Ready?"

Peter and Mama picked up their bags and we all set out again. It was still, the silence broken occasionally by the eerie cry of some unknown animal. More than ever I wanted to be home in my bed, with all my belongings around me. But I trudged on, trying to stay close to Mama. Would the German patrols have a big dog? I was terrified of big dogs. One had bitten me badly when Nanny and I were in the park across from our house and I'd never forgotten it.

I was so worried by the prospect of a dog that I didn't notice the rock until I tripped over it. My foot twisted sharply. I cried out in pain.

Papa turned. "What's wrong?" His voice was quiet.

"I hurt my right ankle."

"*Dummkopf*," muttered Peter.

Bibi heard him. "Anyone could trip," she whispered comfortingly.

Papa came over and ran his hands over it. "You've sprained it. Hard to say how badly." He undid his scarf and wrapped it tightly around my ankle. "This will help to reduce the swelling. Try and keep as much weight off that foot as possible. Bibi, help your brother walk. We'll have a doctor look at it once we get to Holland."

Mama gave me a little hug. "It's been a big day and you've been so brave, Käfer. You've all been brave. Just a while longer and then you can rest."

Once more, we set off. Papa used the flashlight now and again to light the way. My ankle ached but I limped along as quickly as I could, leaning against Bibi.

We weren't too far from the light when we heard furious barking and spied a dog running fast toward us. A German patrol! I screamed, but no sound came out.

"Don't run," said Papa. "Stand perfectly still." He didn't need to tell me that. I was rooted to the spot.

Mama dropped the bags. She took my hand and Bibi's and squeezed them hard. We all held our breath.

31

As the dog came closer, Papa suddenly shone the flashlight in its face and shouted, "Go home."

The dog, a German shepherd, ground to a halt, a few feet away from us, still barking, though not as much. Papa repeated loudly, "Go home." The dog looked around, uncertain about what to do.

Up behind him strode a very tall, muscular man, dressed in coveralls. His long-sleeved shirt was rolled up to his elbows. He carried a rifle. "Sit, Adolf." The dog did as he was commanded.

"He wouldn't have attacked you unless I told him to," the man said, his rifle trained on us. "What are you doing in my field in the middle of the night?"

"Our motor car broke down," replied Papa. His voice was even. But he clenched and unclenched one fist.

"Why didn't you stay put until daylight and then get help?"

Papa gave him a long, assessing look. "I think you know why."

The man's eyes narrowed. He stared back for several moments. My heart pounded, and my ankle throbbed. He shifted his gun. My stomach knotted.

The silence became almost unbearable. Then, as Adolf started to whine, the man finally spoke. Surprisingly, he said, "I have no love for the Führer either." He pointed at the dog. "I named him before Hitler became chancellor. Come, you can stay the rest of the night with my wife and me and I'll take you across the border in the morning, before the sun rises."

We followed him to the farmhouse. The room we entered was homey, with a low ceiling. It was sparsely furnished. A wooden table and chairs stood along one wall. There was a sofa opposite. Two oil lamps provided all the light. In the centre of the room stood a big stone hearth. Bacon and sausages hung above it. The farmer's wife was up, waiting for him. Her face was plain but kind. She took one look at us and silently put more wood on the fire. She didn't ask any questions—did she often have strangers appear in the middle of the night?—but made us cocoa and heated a big pail of water. She handed us face towels and we all washed up quickly in the kitchen sink. Then she showed us to our bedroom. There were two beds covered with rough wool blankets. The sheets and pillows were fresh smelling, though, and it felt good to rest my ankle. Mama, Bibi, and I shared one bed, Papa and Peter the other. It was strange to all sleep in the same room.

"Do you think he's telling the truth, Rifat?" asked Mama very quietly.

"I do. Now let's all try and get some rest. We've been up for hours and tomorrow is another big day."

The farmer—his name was Lange—woke us just as the sun was coming up over the horizon. His wife, he said, was in the barn, milking the cows. They were mooing loudly. Herr Lange led us to his truck, which was filled with bales of straw. He had taken some out to make a hidey-hole for us.

"Lie down under the bales and stay still. With any luck, we won't encounter a patrol. If we do, I've got a story prepared. If they find you, though, you're on your own."

"Why are you doing this for us?" Mama asked quietly. "It's dangerous for you."

Herr Lange's eyes were sad. "My sister is married to a Jew," he said. "He's a good man. A good provider. I don't agree with Hitler."

"And Frau Lange?"

He hesitated. "She worries. She's not so sure we should be helping people—you are not the first—but she won't tell on you."

"Thank you," was all Mama said. There it was again. Hitler didn't like Jews. And Herr Lange seemed to think we were Jews. I wanted to ask Mama why, but I knew now was not the time.

Papa opened his suitcase, took out a leather folder and tucked it under his arm. I recognized it right away. It contained part of his stamp collection. Herr Lange boosted me into the back, along with Bibi and Peter. Papa came last. Once we were settled under the bales, Herr Lange covered everything with a tarp, got in the front beside Adolf, and started the engine.

We bumped along through the field, coming ever closer to the border, which he'd told us wasn't far. We couldn't see anything. It was hard to breathe because there wasn't much air, and the hay, though it smelled like mown grass, was scratchy on my face. My ankle throbbed.

"Halt!" It was a command.

We came to an abrupt stop. I found Bibi's hand in the dark. It was clammy like mine.

"Your identification papers," someone—a border patrol I assumed—ordered tersely.

A pause. Then a rustle.

"Where are you going?"

"I'm taking straw to a farmer who needs it. He's just on the other side of the border. He and I help each other out all the time." Herr Lange was matter of fact.

"Let me look under that tarp." Through a crack in the bales, I saw the soldier whip it off and walk down the side of the truck. I shrank under the hay bale, my heart in my throat. Bibi and I held on fast to each other's hands.

"All right," the soldier said finally. "You can't cross without going through border control any more. I'll let it go this time."

I squeezed Bibi's hand even tighter.

"Wait, what have we here?" he said suddenly. He banged the bale next to ours. "Come out," he commanded.

I froze. We all did. Papa crawled out from under it and jumped down beside the soldier.

At that moment, a stalk of hay scratched my nose and I felt a big sneeze coming on. I pinched my nostrils hard, willing myself to stifle it.

"Check to see if he's alone."

"Achoo!" Quick as a flash, I let go of Bibi's hand and slipped out from under the same bale Papa had. Maybe the soldiers would think there was just Papa and me and not search for the others.

"Achoo! Achoo!" I stood on the straw, favouring my left leg and looked down at them. I wiped my runny nose with the sleeve of my coat.

They were both young and cocky. One of them had a wonky eye, so it was hard to tell where he was looking. The other had a crooked nose that looked like it had been broken. Both had blonde hair, though Crooked Nose's was stringy and thinning at the front.

"Ah, so you're not on your own," said Wonky Eye. He had been doing all the talking. His hand was steady as he trained his gun on Papa. "Is there anyone else?"

"No," said Papa. His voice was sad. "Just my son Heinz and me. He needs medical attention for his ankle."

I stared at Wonky Eye forlornly.

"And you knew about them?" This was directed at Herr Lange.

He shook his head. "Never seen them before."

"Show me your papers," he said to Papa.

"We don't have our papers with us," said Papa. "But, if you let us go, I will give you this."

His stamp collection! That was why Papa had taken it out of his suitcase. He opened it now and showed it to Wonky Eye.

"Stamps?" he asked dismissively.

"These are all first editions and in mint condition," Papa explained. "They're worth a small fortune. Take them and let us cross the border. We're just two people. We're nothing to you."

Crooked Nose approached and peered at them.

35

"I had a stamp collection when I was younger, Horst. Nothing like these. These are valuable." He paused and turned the page, his eyes widening. "Ingrid's pregnant again. We could use the money. I say, let's take them."

A pause, as Wonky Eye thought about it. "I don't like it," he said.

"No one needs to know," argued Crooked Nose.

"Our job is to arrest people trying to cross the border illegally. Like these two."

"And we get paid a pittance for it. Are you so rich you couldn't use the money we could get from these stamps?" Crooked Nose glanced over at Papa and me. "Look at them. They're pathetic. And the boy does look like he needs a doctor."

"You're too soft. We could take the stamps and still turn them in," said Wonky Eye.

Crooked Nose just stared at him.

Wonky Eye took another excruciating moment to make up his mind. I held my breath until, with a heavy sigh, he grabbed the folder out of Papa's hand.

"Get back in and go," he ordered Papa. "And, you, farmer, be more careful in the future. You're lucky I'm feeling generous this morning. Smuggling Jews across the border could get you sent to a camp."

While Papa climbed back up, I sat down on the bale to shield the others from prying eyes. There it was again. Jews. Why did Wonky Eye assume we were Jewish? We didn't look so different from him and Crooked Nose.

Less than a minute later, Herr Lange announced, "We're in Holland." He spoke loudly enough that Mama, Peter, and Bibi heard. They poked their heads out, picked hay out of their hair, and brushed it off their coats.

"That was quick thinking, Käfer." Papa smiled and gave me a pat on the back.

Herr Lange took us right to the *Gasthaus* in the Dutch town. When we'd all climbed down from the truck, Papa retrieved a second leather folder from his suitcase. He handed it to Herr Lange. "This is for you. It's the other half of my stamp collection."

"I can't take it."

"Please. You risked your life to save ours. It's a small thank you, all things considered."

Part Two

The Hague, May 1940

Chapter 5

Today is a birthday, hooray, hooray
I clearly can tell it is yours.
We all are so happy for you and so
we'll sing this song for you.
We wish you many years, hooray
we wish you many years, hooray
we wish you many years, hooray
yes many years, hooray!

It was May 1. My birthday. I took a deep breath and focused on the ten candles on my cake. It was a *slagroomtaart*, my favourite, with layers of cake, whipped cream, and fresh fruit. Mama had invited seven of my school friends—plus Bibi and Peter, to make ten—and we were gathered at the dining-room table. *Whoosh*. I blew them all out in one breath. Everyone clapped. Mama began to cut slices and hand them around.

My party was almost over. The best part was when we played *spijkerpoepen*. Mama and Anika, our cook, had tied a string with a nail to each person's trouser bottoms and we'd competed to see who would be the first to get the nail into a narrow bottle. After a lot of wiggling and laughing my best friend Thijs won. He was the tallest of us all and the best at games. Horst, who was clumsy and almost never won, came in second. After that, I opened my presents under the linden tree in the garden. It wasn't nearly as big as our garden in Berlin—neither was the house—but I liked that all the houses on our street lined up in a cozy row, like friends on a bench.

And my birthday wasn't over yet. I would get my big gift from Father and Mama later, when Father got home from work. I was pretty sure what it was, too. A brand-new bicycle!

Then, tomorrow, my class was going on a trip to the Royal Picture Gallery Mauritshuis to see paintings by the great Dutch masters. I had seen them before on visits to the gallery with Mama, but I could never look at them long enough. Best of all, I wouldn't have to sit in an airless classroom all day.

Thijs was the last to leave my party.

"Pick you up tomorrow at eight?" he said as he laced up his shoes.

"Yes!" I nodded happily. We walked to school every day and shared secrets.

Thijs wasn't excited about the class trip—he liked math and science, which is why Father thought so well of him—but he agreed it would be nice to be away from school for the day. I waved goodbye and watched him walk down the street, his blonde head bobbing to some song he was singing.

"Did you have a good time, Käfer?" Mama asked when he was gone and Anika and her sister Mila were cleaning up. We only had the two of them now to help around the house and they didn't live in like Nanny and Fritz. I liked it better because I saw more of Mama.

"It was the best birthday I've ever had," I assured her.

Mama laughed and gave me a kiss. "Papa and I have a surprise for you later. Take your presents up to your room now and put them away. Then do your homework. I'll call you when Papa gets home."

I was studying the instruction manual for the new Agfa camera that Bibi and Peter had given me when Bibi wandered into my room.

"What are you doing, Käfer?"

"Reading about how to use my camera. How did you know I wanted one?"

"You mentioned it a while ago and I remembered."

42

"I think I know how to work it." I closed the manual and laid it on the bed. "Sit here on the window seat in the light and I'll take your picture."

Bibi sat, legs crossed, and smiled at the camera. I looked through the viewfinder. It took me a moment to focus on her head and shoulders. There she was! I saw every feature clearly. Her heart-shaped face. Curly brown hair hanging over her shoulders in two plaits. Dark eyes under dark brows. *Click.* The camera gave me a whole new way to look at the world and I was hooked instantly.

"I think that will turn out really well!" I said excitedly. "Let's try another. Turn your head a bit, don't look at the camera, and be serious this time." Bibi did as I directed. I stepped closer, so just her face was in the lens. As she gazed straight ahead, her eyes focused on something in the distance, I hesitated for a moment, struck by her expression. She seemed older somehow. And more confident. As if she knew things I didn't. *Click.* I documented her twelve-year-old likeness forever.

"I think you like being a director." She smiled, back to the Bibi I knew.

"I guess I do." I realized I liked the feeling of being in charge.

"I wish we could see the photographs right away," she said and then, "Are you excited about your present from Papa and Mama?"

I nodded. Excited and apprehensive at the same time. I worried I wouldn't be able to ride a bicycle. Especially with Father supervising.

"Don't worry, it's not that hard." Bibi could always read my thoughts. You'll catch on quickly."

I wasn't so sure. I sat on my bed. "But what if I don't? Nothing I do is ever good enough for Father." I looked at my camera sadly.

"That's not true," she said, but we both knew it was. I'd impressed Father once, a long time ago when we left Germany. But since we'd moved to The Hague, we'd slipped back into our old ways and I couldn't seem to recapture his approval.

43

Bibi quickly changed the subject. "You know what I was thinking? I don't miss Berlin anymore."

"I don't either. I miss Aunt Charlotte, though, and sometimes Nanny. And I miss going to the Zoo with Mama, and to Herr Meier's, but I like it here."

"I miss Aunt Charlotte, too. I wonder why she hasn't come to visit." Bibi looked thoughtful. "She didn't send you a birthday present either, did she? That's strange. She always does."

I nodded my head. We all looked forward to Aunt Charlotte's presents. She had a knack for finding just the right thing for everyone. Mama said it was because she paid attention to what interested people.

"Remember that sketch set she gave you?"

Bibi smiled at the memory. "I drew her a little portrait of her friend Luise in charcoal. Aunt Charlotte had it framed and hung it on the wall in her living room so all her friends would see it when they came to visit."

"And she sent me that flashlight last year so I could read in bed at night without Mama knowing!" I had used it to finish reading *Emil and the Detectives*.

That was after we'd moved to The Hague. The last time I had actually been with Aunt Charlotte was one afternoon at home just before we left Berlin. Everyone else, including Nanny, was either out or busy and I was at loose ends. Aunt Charlotte suddenly appeared at the front door dressed in wide-legged khaki trousers and a loose white blouse tucked in at the waist.

"Why the long face, Käfer?" she asked in her smoky voice. She knelt down on one knee and looked right at me with sympathetic hazel eyes. Her wavy auburn hair was parted on the side and pulled back straight from her face.

"Nobody has time to play with me."

"I do!"

"Can we play hide and seek?"

"I'll count to fifty while you go and hide."

"Anywhere?"

"Anywhere in the house."

She turned and started counting. I smiled to myself. I knew exactly where I was going to hide. I raced up to the nursery, slamming the bathroom door on the way to make it seem like that was where I was headed, and grabbed all the stuffed animals. Then I got into Bibi's bed, making myself as small as possible, and arranged them so they covered me. Aunt Charlotte would never think of looking for me there!

"Ready or not, here I come," I heard her call.

She climbed the stairs all the way up. "I wonder if he's in the bathroom," she said, as I tried not to giggle. "Not there. Hmm." She walked across the hallway to the nursery. "Maybe he's in the cupboard." She opened the door and peered in. "The curtain?" She swept it back. "Under the bed?" She got down on her knees and peered underneath Bibi's bed. "Where could my little nephew be?"

Aunt Charlotte plopped herself down beside me and I giggled out loud. She tossed the toys aside. I was kind of happy to be found because I was hot and sweaty.

"There you are! What a splendid hiding spot. Oh, you are an imaginative boy. And I am the luckiest aunt in all of Berlin."

"The luckiest aunt in all of Germany," I corrected her. She laughed as she wrapped me in a hug and kissed the top of my head. "Time for a treat. I heard the ice cream cart in the park just now."

Bibi put a hand on my shoulder, drawing me back. "Käfer, what are you thinking?"

"About Aunt Charlotte. And how she always has time for us. I miss her."

"I know Mama and Papa are worried about her. They want her to come and live here."

"She should," I said. "We haven't seen her in so long. We could do things together, like we did in Berlin." I got excited thinking about it.

"Maybe she can't move here. Maybe it's hard for her to leave. Remember how it was for us?"

How could I forget? I still sometimes had nightmares about the angry crowd in front of the shop in Berlin. The threatening lieutenant at the *Gasthaus*. Adolf barking in the farmer's field. Mama would hear me crying out and come in to my room and read to me until I went back to sleep.

"And remember when we first got here?" Bibi persisted.

I did. We'd been in The Hague for more than two years and it felt like home now. But I could still recall how hard it was at first to understand what people were saying and how different a lot of the food was. Especially the *haring*. I still hadn't acquired a taste for slurping down raw herring. Thijs teased me about it. I wasn't really Dutch, he said. Thinking about it now, I wasn't sure what I was. Dutch? German? Jewish?

"I like it here," I declared. "I like my school and my friends. I like having a room to myself, even if it is small. And I like that I can look out over the city to the sea."

"Me, too, though I miss talking to you before I fall asleep at night, Käfer."

I loved Bibi. She was a lot like Aunt Charlotte.

Daylight was fading by the time Father got home from work. His eyes had a distracted look that meant his mind was somewhere else. It made me nervous.

He wheeled out my new bicycle. It was a Gazelle! Black frame and seat. Just what I'd asked for.

"Thank you, Mama. Thank you, Father," I said.

"Time to learn to ride it," Father said briskly. "Let's use the path in the boulevard."

Why couldn't we be in the garden where no one could see?

We all marched across the street except for Peter. He was in his room making a model plane. He planned to surprise Father with it.

Father held the bicycle steady. Although there were few people out, and trees lined both sides of the path, I felt eyes bore into me from second-floor windows up and down the street. I took a deep breath and got on.

"Put your feet on the pedals. Now start pedalling." I did as I was told. Father pushed me, then ran alongside, holding me upright. Suddenly, he wasn't there. The bike wobbled and before I knew it, down it went, me along with it.

Mama and Bibi ran over. "Are you all right, Käfer?"

I'd scraped my knee—not badly enough that it tore my trousers— and it hurt, but I shook my head. I didn't want Father to know.

"Try again," he said.

He held the bicycle upright while I got back on, and when he told me to, I started pedalling. Mama and Bibi cheered me on. Father gave me a push, but I lost my balance and fell again.

"Once more, Heinz." Father's voice was impatient. My hands started to sweat, and my knees trembled. I just wanted to go inside and try again tomorrow. But I obeyed and crashed almost immediately.

"Don't worry, Käfer, you'll learn soon enough," said Mama, as I got up. She helped me pick up my bicycle.

"He will know how to ride by the time I get home from work tomorrow, or the bicycle goes back to the shop," said Father.

Mama looked at him in surprise. "Don't be so hard on him, Rifat," she chided gently.

"You baby him, Else. He needs to get tougher. Life is full of hard knocks and it takes more than charm to succeed."

Mama gave him a wry smile and let it go. "I'll ask Peter to help you learn tomorrow after school," she said to me.

"No, Mama, Thijs said he would teach me." I hadn't actually asked him, but I was certain I didn't want Peter's help. I'd rather give back my bicycle.

"That's a better idea," she agreed. "Now put your bicycle away and you two go upstairs and finish your homework. I'll be up shortly."

But it wasn't Mama who arrived upstairs about half an hour later. It was Father who appeared in the doorway of Peter's room.

Bibi and I were watching him construct a Spitfire bomber out of sheet metal and wire. He'd first drawn the outline of the plane on paper; then, with scissors, he had cut the parts out of sheet metal Father had brought home from work. Now he was gluing them onto the fuselage. It was very clever, and Bibi and I were captivated. Which meant there wasn't time for me to escape back to my own room and avoid Father. My heart sank.

"What have we here?" Father asked. He walked over to Peter's desk.

Peter looked up and pushed back his forelock. "A model Spitfire." His voice cracked. It had been doing that a lot the last few months.

"He's going to paint it later so it will look like a real plane, only miniature," explained Bibi. "Isn't it ingenious, Papa? When he's finished, he's going to make a U-boat for Ernst. You know, Papa, a German submarine. See, he's already done a drawing." She held the paper up for Father to see. With a long, rounded hull and finlike periscope, the U-boat resembled a whale.

"So that's what the scrap sheet metal was for! Very well done, Peter. You're gifted with your hands," said Father. He picked up the Spitfire model and admired it. I started to back out of the room slowly so as not to attract his attention and remind him of what a failure I was.

But Father turned suddenly and caught my eye. I froze. He put the plane back down on Peter's desk and walked past me to the window. "I haven't been up here in a long time. I'd forgotten what a wonderful view you have. Look, there's Noordeinde Palace. The Queen is likely having dinner right now. And over there in the distance is Ypenburg airfield. Remember when I took you boys there with me on business? What was that, a few months ago?"

He turned and looked at me again. I nodded. "And we went to Ockenburg before that," remembered Peter.

"That's right, we did." Father turned back to the view. "And you can see the North Sea too. But it's getting late, time for all of you to get ready for bed. Mama will be up to say good night shortly."

With that, Father gave Bibi a hug and a kiss, and me a pat on the back. It was his way of saying he felt bad for being hard on me earlier.

I slept fitfully that night. The next morning, my first thought was how I'd kept falling off my bicycle and how disappointed Father had been. Then I remembered the class trip and cheered up. I got dressed quickly and hurried down to breakfast. Father was reading the newspaper.

He looked up briefly. "Tuck in your shirt properly, Heinz."

Mama gave me a smile. "Eat up, Käfer. Thijs will be here soon. He's always on time."

"He is, and he's clever at math and science," said Father without taking his eyes off his paper. "He's a good friend for you, Heinz. You can learn a lot from him."

"And he can learn to appreciate history and art from you, Käfer." Mama patted my hand.

As I wolfed down my bread topped with *appelstroop*, there was a knock at the front door.

"That will be Thijs," I said, jumping up.

"Ask him to come in for a moment," said Father.

I ran to open the door. Thijs stood there looking tall and composed. His curly blonde hair had been carefully combed. His shirt was tucked neatly into his trousers.

"Step in. My father wants to see you," I said. Thijs looked surprised but nodded his head. He followed me into the dining room, both of us wondering what Father would say.

"Ah, Thijs, good morning," Father said pleasantly. He put down his newspaper and took a sip of his coffee. "Are you still interested in learning about aeroplanes and how they work?"

"Oh, yes, Meneer Avigdor."

"I'll take you and Heinz to one of the airfields soon—perhaps next week—and we'll go on a tour."

"Thank you!" Thijs said excitedly. His bright blue eyes shone. "Do you think we can fly in an aeroplane?" I held my breath. I'd always wanted to see what it was like to be up in the sky looking down at the landscape, even if I didn't much care about the mechanics of it all.

Father's smile included both of us. "We can ask." Knowing Father, the answer would be "yes."

On the way to school, as we walked past rows of identical three-storey, red-brick townhouses and breathed in the fresh salt smell of the North Sea, Thijs couldn't stop talking about going to the airfield. Finally, I was able to tell him what Father had said about taking my bicycle back to the shop and asked if he would help me learn to ride it after school.

"Of course I will. You'll pick it up quickly with me teaching you. And I'll show you how to fix a flat tire. Everyone who rides a bicycle should know how to do that."

When we got to the Royal Picture Gallery Mauritshuis, I forgot all about my bicycle. I couldn't take my eyes off the paintings. They were works by famous Dutch masters like Rembrandt and

Rubens and they were very realistic. My favourite was *Girl with a Turban* by Johannes Vermeer. It reminded me of Mama's painting by Botticelli, *Portrait of a Young Woman,* which had hung on the wall in our house in Berlin. Before it disappeared. I wondered if Mama would ever tell me what had happened to it.

I stared at the painting for a long time, drawn by the expression on the girl's face. As I stood there, I became aware of a girl standing beside me. She was equally mesmerized.

On impulse, I turned to her. Her dark hair and eyes and heart-shaped face reminded me of Bibi. She had a journal in her hand and I could see she had been writing in it. I looked back at the painting. "It's like she's looking right at you," I ventured.

The girl nodded. "As if we'd just caught her attention. I'm so glad to have seen her." There was something final in the way she said it.

"You can always come back."

She shook her head. "I live in Amsterdam. I'm on a school trip. Are you from here?"

I nodded. "We moved from Berlin two years ago."

"We came from Frankfurt," she said. "I was only four, though, so I don't remember much about it."

"You're lucky. I missed Berlin for a long time after we got here. I like The Hague now, but I didn't at first. Everything was so strange. And we didn't know anyone, except my parents' friends. We lived with them in their house before we got our own and we had to be perfectly behaved all the time." I had a sudden memory of Mama asking me to take tea plates from the table to the kitchen at the Berkovitchs' and me replying, "But the maid does that." Mama gave me a look that conveyed, in no uncertain terms, life had changed.

"Why did you come here?" the girl asked.

"My Father said it was getting too dangerous to live in Germany."

"That's why we moved, too."

I wanted to ask her if she was Jewish, but it seemed too personal. Instead, I said, "Do you like living in Amsterdam?"

51

"Yes. I have lots of friends and I love my school." We heard a clapping sound and she looked toward the exit. "I have to go now. That's my teacher." She put out her hand. "It's been nice talking to you. My name is Anne."

"I'm Heinz. Heinz Avigdor."

"I will always remember meeting a Heinz Avigdor," she smiled, revealing slightly crooked front teeth. "And who knows? Maybe we'll see each other again." And then she was gone.

With Thijs' help, I learned to ride my Gazelle. It didn't take long. He told me to "lean into the pedals" and I took off. A bit wobbly at first, but within minutes I was riding steadily. It felt so liberating! The harder I pedalled, the faster I went. Why hadn't I learned to cycle before? I couldn't wait to show Father. He'd let me keep my bicycle now.

Before Thijs went home, I got him to sit on his bicycle and lean forward, one foot on a pedal, as if he was pushing off. I gazed through the viewfinder. He looked windblown and carefree. *Click.*

I went into the house. Anika told me Mama was out, so I decided to wait for her in the drawing room so I could tell her all about my triumph the moment she arrived home. I curled up on a sofa and before I knew it, I fell asleep.

I was wakened by the sound of voices. I recognized them immediately. Father and his partner Herr Berkovitch. They were talking in Father's office, which was just off the drawing room. I lay still.

"I think we'll need to leave The Hague soon and join you in England, Bernhard," Father was saying.

We were going to move? Again? My heart started to pound.

"Austria, Czechoslovakia, Poland, how much longer before Hitler sends his army across the border into Holland?" Father continued. "Neutrality doesn't matter to a man like that."

"You're right about Hitler," said Herr Berkovitch. "It's high time you and Else and the children moved, Rifat. The British are eager to get your fuel pump into production and you need to be there to supervise."

"I also have some new information for them on aircraft production in Germany."

"Another good reason to get out of Holland now. You're already a wanted man in Germany and if Hitler finds out you've been supplying intelligence to the British—"

Intelligence? Did that mean Father was a spy? My heart beat faster.

There was a short silence. "Will you tell the children in advance this time?" Herr Berkovitch asked.

"They're old enough now to know. Peter has been telling me what his friends at school say about Hitler." Father paused. "I don't think Ellen or Heinz are aware of what's happening. They're too young to read the newspapers and we've shielded them. But that can't continue much longer."

"You'll have to caution them to stay quiet, Rifat. Most Dutch don't care for Hitler, but there are Nazis here."

Another silence.

Then Papa said, "It was Ursula who betrayed us in Berlin."

"Ursula?"

"Our maid. I later discovered she was a Gestapo informer. I should have listened to Else. She was suspicious of Ursula from the start and didn't want me to hire her."

Then Herr Berkovitch asked, "Where is Else?"

"She went to send a telegram to her sister."

"I take it there's been no word from Charlotte?"

"Not for many weeks." Father's voice sounded worried. "And she didn't send a present for Heinz's birthday. Lotte wouldn't forget that. She adores Heinz. The last we heard she was making plans to come here. That was months ago. Else is sick with worry.

There are so many stories of people just 'disappearing' in Germany and what she was doing was more dangerous than—"

Father cut himself off. "Ah, here's Else now," he said.

Mama had come in so quietly I hadn't heard her cross the vestibule and go into Father's office, drawn by the sound of his and Herr Berkovitch's voices.

"Bernhard, how nice to see you." Mama sounded awfully tired.

"The pleasure is mine, Else. I'm glad you arrived home before I had to leave. But now, I really must go. Let me know about your plans, Rifat."

There were sounds of footsteps as Mama and Father walked Herr Berkovitch to the front door and said goodbye.

"Give our best to Margarethe," Mama said.

"I will. I leave for England in the morning. I hope we'll see you in London soon."

The door closed.

"Were you able to send the telegram?" Father asked.

"Yes, although the lineup was long." Mama's voice was so sad. "I've almost lost hope I'll get a reply. She hasn't responded to any of my other telegrams. She seems to have vanished. I fear I'll never see her again."

When they were safely in Father's office with the door closed, I got up quietly and slowly climbed the stairs to the third floor. Peter's bedroom door was shut, which meant he didn't want to be disturbed. Bibi was at her desk doing homework. She looked up.

"Did you learn to ride your bicycle?" she asked.

I paused just outside her doorway and nodded.

"Good for you, Käfer," she said.

I continued down the hall to my room. I needed to think about what I had just overheard before I said anything to Bibi. If I told her at all. I didn't want her to lecture me about eavesdropping. It's not like I'd had much choice. Father and Herr Berkovitch had been in the middle of a conversation when I woke up. There was no way I could have left the drawing room without them noticing me.

I took Funny Bunny Blue from under my pillow and hugged him as I sank down onto the window seat. I curled up and stared out at the boulevard just across the way. It was lined with linden trees starting to bud. In another month, the air would be filled with their sweet smell. But we wouldn't be here then. We would be in England.

Could Father really be a spy for the British? He knew a lot about aeroplanes, so I guess it was possible. And it would explain why we had to leave Berlin so quickly without telling anyone. Maybe it didn't have anything to do with being Jewish after all. If we were even Jewish, a topic Father and Mama avoided talking about. Maybe Hitler didn't like Father because he had invented that fuel pump—something that could help win the war—and then sold it to the British. Come to think of it, Father had gone to England twice since we'd moved to The Hague. And, both times, he'd been unusually cheerful when he'd returned.

And Father had said that what Aunt Charlotte was doing was dangerous. But what could that possibly be?

I turned it over in my mind until my head hurt, but I couldn't come up with any answers. As I gazed unseeingly out the window, the harsh chatter of starlings down the street invaded my thoughts. Quiet at first, the unmistakable mix of warbles, whistles, and rattles grew in volume as more of the noisy birds joined the flock, heading home to roost for the night. I didn't like them. There was something menacing about their dark, glossy bodies and sharp yellow beaks and the way they swarmed by the hundreds overhead.

Mama called to say it was time for dinner. I got up and closed the window, shutting out the din.

Chapter 6

Peter, Bibi, and I were all doing our homework when Father summoned us to his office. Mama was sitting in a wing chair listening to the radio. Father was behind his desk, which was covered with papers as usual. He looked up and pushed them aside as we entered. Mama turned off the radio.

Father got straight to the point.

"We are moving to England. And very soon. But you are to tell no one." It was like Berlin all over again.

I opened my mouth to ask Father why, but Peter beat me to it.

"Why, Father? Why do we have to move again?" He pushed back his forelock. His voice had an aggressive edge to it. I'd never heard Peter speak that way to Father before. From the surprised look on his face, it was clear that neither had Father, although he kept his temper.

"Because it's not going to be safe for us here much longer, Peter. You know Hitler is on the march across Europe. You've talked about it with some of your friends. And with me."

But not with me, I thought.

"Shouldn't we stay and fight him? Stand up to him? That's what you told me to do with bullies, and isn't he a bully?"

Father looked exasperated.

"Well, isn't he?" said Peter, his voice cracking. His face flushed. "Why do you always have to run? From Constantinople to Berlin. Berlin to The Hague. Now from The Hague to England, and who knows where after that?"

"I didn't 'run' from Constantinople. I went to Berlin to get an education and stayed because I met your Mother." Father's voice was dangerously quiet as he stood and came around to the front of his desk. "I've had to work hard for everything I've achieved. You don't know anything, Peter. You've led a sheltered life."

Peter didn't back down. If anything, Father's words seemed to enrage him even more.

"And whose fault is that?" he shouted. "I'm not a child anymore. Even if you treat me like one. I don't want to go to England. I'm Dutch now. I want to stay here and join a resistance group. That's what Ernst is going to do if Hitler invades Holland."

"Ah, you and your good friend Ernst have talked about that, have you? And you both want to end up as your Aunt Charlotte most likely has? That's not the future I have in mind for you."

Mama gasped. Bibi and I looked at each other in dismay.

"What do you mean?" asked Peter. "Aunt Charlotte is in Berlin. Working in an automobile factory."

"You know we haven't heard from her in months, Peter." Father paused. He looked pained. "What you don't know is that she was spying for people opposing Hitler."

Aunt Charlotte a spy?

At first, Peter was too stunned to say anything. Then he blurted out, "But what would *she* be able to tell them?"

"Think about it. You want to be in the resistance. Automobile factories make military vehicles as well as passenger motor cars. Your aunt had access to information of great interest to the Allies. Before we left Berlin, your Mother and I told her it was getting too dangerous to keep passing it on. To get out with us. But she didn't listen."

I glanced at Mama. She sat straight in the chair, her eyes bright with unshed tears.

"Where is she?" Peter sounded worried, not angry, anymore.

Father sighed and went back around the desk. He sat down heavily. "I don't know, but I think it's likely she's in a detention camp. There's no sense in hiding it from you any longer." His face was sad.

"What's a detention camp, Papa?" I asked.

"It's a place where Hitler sends people who don't agree with him." I frowned. "What happens there?"

"No one knows for sure, Heinz. There are rumours, but people aren't often released from the camps. They're very bad places."

We were all silent as we tried to digest what that could mean.

"At least she *did* something," said Peter finally, though he didn't sound as certain as he had. "She fought. She didn't run away. Like you did. We did."

"Stop, Peter," said Mama, standing up. Her voice was sharp. "Your Father is right. You don't know what you're talking about. Now, all of you, go to your rooms. I don't want to listen to another word."

I tried to read for a while, but I had trouble concentrating. Finally, I turned off the light and tried to sleep. But I couldn't do that either. I tossed and turned and eventually got out of bed, intending to go across the hall to Bibi's room and talk about what had happened between Father and Peter. But then I heard Mama coming up the stairs. I slipped back under the covers as she went in to say good night to Peter. She was in his room for a long while. Then she went to Bibi's room.

Finally, she opened my bedroom door. I could smell her perfume. It was Vol de Nuit. The bottle looked a bit like a spinning aeroplane propeller. Mama had worn that same scent for as long as I could remember, and I loved it. It was exotic and comforting at the same time. Like Mama.

She walked over to my bed. The light from the hall shone on both our faces. I knew I looked as unhappy as I felt.

"You're upset by what happened tonight, aren't you?" she said.

I nodded. She sat down beside me.

"Everything is going to be fine, Käfer. You mustn't worry. But you must try to understand the pressure Papa is under to make sure we're safe and have a future." She paused. "And it's not just us who depend on Papa. He helps to take care of your Grandmother Avigdor in Constantinople and your two aunts in Rome. So, you see, there are many people who rely on him."

"But, Peter—"

"Peter knows he behaved badly. What could he be thinking? The resistance at thirteen! It's preposterous."

"And Aunt Charlotte—"

"All we can do is pray and hope for the best. We don't know anything for certain and your aunt is very strong and brave and resourceful." Mama paused. "So is your papa. He's also very clever. And, although he doesn't show it often, he loves you very much, Käfer." With that, Mama got up and left my room, closing the door softly behind her.

I didn't doubt that Father loved me. But I wanted him to be proud of me. Despite my best efforts, I was a disappointment to him. I knew it for certain. I'd known it since I was six.

It had been a warm summer evening and Father and Herr Berkovitch were sitting in the garden at the house in Berlin. Talking about business as they always did. Peter, Bibi, and I were playing nearby.

Suddenly, Herr Berkovitch, who was watching us, asked Father, "Will the boys follow in your footsteps?"

Father didn't hesitate, "Peter will. He's got the brain of an engineer. Heinz doesn't. I don't know what he will do."

Every time I remembered that moment, I got a knot in my stomach.

The next week was agony. Peter and Father's argument—brief though it had been—lingered in the air. All of us avoided saying anything about leaving Holland and, as Papa had directed, we didn't mention it to anyone. At school, everyone was suddenly talking about the Germans and whether it was true German troops were building at the border. And at night, as I lay in bed, my thoughts inevitably turned to Aunt Charlotte. She couldn't write and tell us how she was. So I wondered. And worried. Did they make her do hard physical work? And if she didn't do what they said, did they punish her with no dinner—or worse yet, hit her? I couldn't even imagine what her life was like now. Aunt Charlotte, who never hurt anyone.

The only time I felt normal was after school when Thijs and I rode our bicycles all over The Hague. I was getting more confident with each passing day. And it was spring. The trees were all in bud and tulips were blooming everywhere. As we flew down one street after another, the salt air fresh in my face, I felt free! And almost happy.

Father worked harder than ever getting ready to leave for England. He came home too late for me to show him how well I could ride. But I knew the time would come when I would surprise him. The opportunity came a week after he and Peter had quarrelled. For once, Father was home in time for dinner and when we had finished eating I asked him if he would like to see me on my bicycle.

He looked a bit surprised—it was clear he'd forgotten all about his ultimatum—but he said, "Yes, show me."

So, I got my Gazelle, and Father stood on the sidewalk in front of our house and watched me race down the street and back. I braked in front of him. He was smiling.

"Well done, Käfer. You've got it now and it's a skill you'll have all of your life. You never know when it will come in handy. Put your bicycle away and come inside. I have something for you."

As I wheeled my bicycle away, my cheeks flushed with pleasure. Father had called me Käfer.

I found Father in his office poring over his aeroplane designs. The radio was on. A cello sonata by Brahms was coming to a close. I recognized it because we'd studied it in music appreciation class not long before. Then the eight o'clock news began. Father signalled me to sit down in the chair across from him and we both listened. I felt very grown up. Father had never invited me to hear the news before.

"Good evening," the announcer began in a solemn voice. "We have confirmed tonight that Denmark and Norway have been occupied by German forces. No significant resistance was offered.

"In the case of Holland, there are unconfirmed reports of a build-up of German forces along the country's eastern border. However, earlier today German Chancellor Adolf Hitler pledged goodwill to the people of the Netherlands."

Then Hitler came on the air. I had never heard him before. His voice rang out in guttural German. "We will never attack the Netherlands. They are our best friends. They're on the west of us to protect Germany from England."

Hitler wasn't going to invade Holland! He'd just promised. Perhaps we wouldn't have to move after all. My heart leapt at the thought.

The announcer returned. "The prime minister will address the nation at nine thirty this evening."

"And he'll tell us there will be no war," said Father. He snapped off the radio. "I don't believe Hitler, and the Prime Minister is a fool if he does."

Father opened up his desk drawer and brought out a gold pocket watch. As he handed it to me, the desk lamp revealed dark circles under his eyes and new lines on his face.

"This belonged to your grandfather Avigdor. I'm sorry you never knew him. He was a fine man. I'm giving it to you now, Käfer, because I want you to have something of his. You've earned it. Your teachers tell Mama that you're a good student and you learned to ride your bicycle. I've cleaned the watch and set the time."

I ran my finger over Grandfather's initials etched into the gold cover. *IA* for Ismael Avigdor. I could hardly believe it. Father had given Peter a few family keepsakes, but this was the first for me.

"Thank you, Papa. I'll take good care of it. I promise."

"See that you do. Now off you go. I've got work to do."

I ran upstairs to show Bibi. She was in Peter's room marvelling at the crystal radio he had almost finished building.

As I burst into the room, Peter was saying, "When it's done, I'll be able to hear the radio whenever I want and find out what's really going on—"

"Look what Papa just gave me," I interrupted. "It was Grandfather Avigdor's."

"That's wonderful, Käfer," Bibi said, admiring it. "It's beautiful."

"So, it's 'Papa' now, is it?" said Peter, looking up from his radio. "Funny how when he's Papa to you, he's Father to me."

I ignored him. "Guess what I heard on the news? Hitler said he would never invade Holland."

"Do you think that means we'll stay?" Bibi asked.

"Probably not," Peter interrupted bitterly. "When Father makes up his mind about something, it's almost impossible to unmake it."

"But this is different," I said. "Hitler promised. I heard him."

"What exactly did he say?" Peter asked, pushing back his forelock and blinking.

"The Germans would never attack Holland. We're their best friends."

"What was Father's response?"

"He said he didn't believe Hitler."

Peter nodded knowingly, as Mama called from the second-floor landing. "You three, it's time to get ready for bed. You've got school tomorrow."

"Can't we stay up a bit later?" I wheedled.

"No. Now." Mama was firm.

Bibi and I obediently went back to our own rooms. I set my new watch on the bedside table so I could look at it if I woke up in the night. Then I put on my pyjamas and went to bed, feeling happier than I had in a week.

Chapter 7

A loud, steady popping sound woke me. I sat up, rubbed my eyes, and turned on my bedside light. I picked up my watch. It was just before four o'clock in the morning. The noise was coming from outside and it was getting louder. I got out of bed, went over to the window, and looked out.

I couldn't believe my eyes. In the light showing up over the horizon, I saw planes—dozens and dozens of them—flying toward the city from the east. They were flying west, toward the sea. They must be going to attack England!

My heart racing, I got my camera and took a few photographs as the bombers drew closer. *Click. Click. Click.* I wasn't sure how the pictures would turn out in the early morning light, but I wanted to try and record what was happening. *Click.*

Bibi ran in to my room. She had thrown on a dressing gown over her pyjamas, but her hair was tousled.

"Käfer, what's happening?" She was breathless.

"Hitler is going to bomb England, I think."

"I hope he doesn't bomb us."

"He won't." I had to shout as the planes grew louder as they came closer. They were definitely German. I could make out the iron cross on their sides. We watched, mesmerized, as wave after wave flew past. Then suddenly, the planes in the distance started turning around over the North Sea and heading back.

"Käfer, look!"

"They're coming back!" Why would that be? Were British bombers chasing them? Or—My throat was dry and my hands on the camera were moist.

As we watched them approach The Hague, they started dropping what looked like small dark eggs that disappeared behind buildings. Suddenly, we saw bright lights as they struck their targets. From the ground, Dutch gunfire answered back. I took a few more photographs. *Click. Click. Click.*

Within moments, we saw a plane start to fall, leaving a trail of fire behind it. It hit the ground with a loud bang—I could feel the reverberations—and more flames leapt into the air. Then another bomber was hit. It, too, spiralled downward. The sky was turning an eerie orange. To the southwest, another firefight broke out between German pilots and Dutch forces on the ground. More planes fell from the sky. It was terrifying and thrilling at the same time. I took another photograph—*click*—wishing my camera could take a really wide shot of the planes soaring, the smoke rising, and the flashes of gunfire coming from both directions.

Bibi tugged at my pyjama top. I tore myself away from the scene outside the window and raced after her downstairs to Mama and Papa's room. They stood on their balcony, their eyes riveted to the sky. Peter stood beside them. By this time, a few Dutch Fokkers were in the air as well.

"Papa, what's happening?"

"You can see for yourself, Käfer," said Papa. "Holland is being invaded by the man who just last night promised never to attack his good friend."

"What does it mean?" Bibi asked.

"We'll be leaving Holland earlier than I'd planned." Papa was strangely calm.

"But won't it be dangerous?" Bibi's voice trembled.

"It would be more dangerous to stay, Schatzi," Papa said softly. He put his arm around her. "Hitler won't be any kinder to the Dutch than he has been to the Poles or the Austrians, or even his fellow Germans."

We all stood and watched the battle unfold around the city. We couldn't tear our eyes away. As yet another wave of German bombers approached, the aircraft doors opened and parachutists started tumbling out and drifting to the ground. There were dozens of them. It was an unforgettable sight. As they fell, leaflets started floating down as well. The sky was white with papers. *Click.*

A piece of paper sailed past the balcony, just out of reach. It landed in the garden below. "I'll fetch it," I volunteered.

When I brought it back upstairs and handed it to Papa, he read it aloud. "Strong German troop units have surrounded the city. Resistance is of no use. Germany does not fight your country, only Great Britain. In order to continue this battle, the German Army has been forced to penetrate your country. The German Army protects the life and goods of every peace-loving citizen. However, German troops will punish every deed of violence with a death sentence." He paused, then he crushed the leaflet in his hand. "Well, we're peace-loving citizens and we have lost nearly everything." His voice was bitter.

"It's like all of Hitler's promises. Not worth the paper it's written on," Mama added, taking his arm.

"Can't we beat Hitler?" Bibi asked.

"No," said Papa. "The Dutch are not well enough prepared. They were lulled into a sense of false security and then betrayed. Come inside. We shouldn't be out here."

Papa closed the balcony door. "I'm going to see if there's any news on the radio."

We all trooped down the stairs after him and followed him into his office. He turned on the set.

Right away we knew. Holland was at war with Germany. Whether we wanted to be or not.

The fighting continued all that day. We could hear it in the distance. Papa said it was centred on the airfields. The Hague itself was strangely quiet for the most part. Still, Mama said we wouldn't go to school. She didn't want us too far from home.

Papa holed up in his office on the telephone, which was still operating. Peter went back to his room and worked on his crystal radio. Bibi decided to do some sketching.

I was restless. I looked for Mama and found her in her room, sitting in a chair by the window. One of her suits and a hat lay on the bed and on the table beside her sat a box filled with loose diamonds. She had pulled several out and started to sew them into the cuff of a pair of Father's trousers. It took me back two years, to that time just before we left Berlin and I saw her stitching an emerald necklace into her dress.

She glanced up as I entered. "You're old enough to know what I'm doing," she said. "We won't be able to take much with us when we leave. But we'll be able to sell these diamonds, and the gold snuff boxes, if need be." She looked over at her collection, which I knew included two gold and enamel Fabergé boxes encrusted with precious gems. She sounded calm, but I knew how much Mama loved them and how hard it would be for her to part with them. They were beautiful and had been gifts from Papa.

"When do we have to leave?"

"Very soon. Papa hopes we'll be able to get out in the next day or two. It depends on how the battle goes."

"I don't want to go. I like it here." I was fighting back tears, but they were falling down my cheeks.

Mama reached over and brushed them away. Her voice was gentle but brisk. "I know, Käfer, but believe me, you don't want to stay. Holland will change just the way Germany did. We can't live like that." She paused. "Think of it as an adventure that we'll all go on together."

I hadn't enjoyed our last "adventure," so that didn't really help.

"What will it be like in England?" I asked, trying to think of something else.

She smiled. "Better than here."

"My English isn't very good."

"You didn't have any Dutch at all when we moved to The Hague and you picked it up in no time! With English, you have a head start as you've been studying it at school. It won't take long for you to speak like an English schoolboy."

I hoped so. "Can I say goodbye to Thijs?"

"No, but you can go and see him now. Just don't stay long. You *mustn't* tell him we're leaving. Papa doesn't want anyone to know. It's safer that way. You can write to Thijs from England and explain."

I didn't really understand why I couldn't tell Thijs we were moving—he was my best friend and we confided everything to each other—but Mama was adamant, so I promised her I wouldn't say anything.

I walked down the street to Thijs'. Everything looked like it always did. A row of handsome red-brick houses. Window boxes filled with brightly coloured tulips. Some people were walking; others riding their bicycles. The bombers were gone and the sun shone. But it felt completely different. As if the city was waiting for something more to happen.

Mevrouw de Groot answered the door, Thijs right behind her. She was cleaning even though, like us, the de Groots had a housekeeper. "I have to do something to keep myself occupied," she said in her singsong voice. She pointed at the rugs she was busy beating, her usually twinkling blue eyes serious. "What's happened is so shocking." I liked Mevrouw de Groot. Like Thijs, she had a ready smile and always made me feel welcome.

As Thijs and I went off to his room, we could hear the "pop, pop, pop" of her carpet beater as she went at the rugs with a vengeance. The sound reminded me of the planes flying past earlier that morning.

"Wasn't it exciting?" Thijs said. He spoke quickly. "All those planes. Paratroopers coming down. And the explosions!"

"Weren't you scared, Thijs?"

"Maybe a little. But mostly it was thrilling."

"I was frightened," I confessed. "And I still am. My father says it's not over and if the Germans win, life in Holland will change a lot. And not for the better."

"My father doesn't think so. He says if we lose, everything will go back to normal quickly because it's the British they're after. Hitler likes us."

"Us?"

"Yes, because we're Aryans."

I looked at Thijs questioningly.

"Members of the master race," he explained impatiently. I knew from the way he said it he was parroting something he'd heard at home. I didn't know exactly what he meant, but I was pretty sure Papa and Mama wouldn't approve.

He was about to continue when his mother came into the room carrying a plate. On it were two big *stroopwafels*. My favourite treat! "What are you boys talking about?" she asked.

"Käfer says his father thinks if the Germans win, things will be different in Holland."

Mevrouw de Groot smiled at me. "Well, it's not a certainty that they will win. I have faith in our Dutch forces. But if the Germans do succeed in occupying Holland, everything will stay the same for *us*, Heinz. You'll see. Have a *stroopwafel*."

As I took one and bit into it, savouring the combination of waffle and caramel, she continued, "It's the Jews I feel sorry for. They must be very worried. The smart ones will try to get out of the country quickly. The Nazis are not kind to Jews."

I felt a stab of fear in my stomach.

"I've got to go home," I said, getting up quickly. "Mama told me not to stay long."

Mevrouw de Groot looked a bit surprised, then nodded. "Take your *stroopwafel* with you, and don't forget, Heinz, Sunday is Mother's Day. Give your mama some tulips."

I didn't say anything to Mama and Papa about what happened at Thijs' and they were both too preoccupied to ask. Mama was still sewing, and Papa was in his office on the telephone.

Upstairs, Bibi and Peter had just put up a long antenna for his radio and Peter was ready to try it out. It didn't look very impressive. Just some wires coiled over a bottle, one wire leading to an antenna, the other to the ground, the earpiece, and a diode wire—that's what Peter called it—all set on a little wooden stand. I didn't see how it could possibly work, but Peter seemed confident. He was smart that way, like Papa.

I went to get my camera as he sat down in front of it, put the earpiece in, and touched a wire to the coil. He shook his head. He moved the wire to another part of the coil. Still nothing. He moved it again. He looked up. His face was bright with excitement. "I can hear music!"

Click! I captured his elation, struck at that moment by how much he looked like Papa.

"Let me hear," said Bibi.

Peter put the earpiece in Bibi's ear. She gasped. "It's wonderful, Peter."

"Can I try?" I asked. I put down my camera. Bibi handed me the earpiece. The sound was faint but clear. Peter really was clever.

"How does it work?" I wanted to know.

"It's simple," Peter said. "The antenna catches the radio waves and the coil allows me to tune the radio to specific stations." I still didn't really understand, and I could tell from Bibi's face she didn't either. All we knew was that it worked.

Peter looked pleased with himself. He reached over for the earpiece. "Let me see if I can find another station," he said.

I handed it back to him. He moved the wire to another part of the coil. Nothing. He moved the wire once more. "I've got another station! It's the news. In English. I'm going to go and tell Papa."

He ran off downstairs. I put the earpiece in and listened. Peter was right. It was an English-speaking station, and I could understand enough to know that the announcer was describing how the Germans had bombed Holland that morning.

"How did it go with Thijs?" Bibi asked, pulling my attention away from the news. "What did he think about the bombers and paratroopers? You didn't tell him what Papa said about moving?"

"No." I looked away and fidgeted with the wire.

Bibi moved so that she could look right at me. "Something happened at Thijs', Käfer. What?"

I swallowed. Bibi could always read my face. "Mevrouw de Groot said even if the Germans did defeat the Dutch, everything in Holland would stay the same because they—we—were Aryans, members of the master race. Hitler wouldn't do anything bad to us." I swallowed again, although my throat was tight. Then I blurted out, "But *we're* not, are we, Bibi? We're Jewish."

"You don't know that, Käfer." I gazed at her. She was right. I didn't know for certain, but I had a feeling we were. And that it wasn't a good thing.

Chapter 8

That night and for the next three nights, Bibi and I went to Peter's room right after dinner. Bibi and I sat on Peter's bed while he located the BBC, England's radio station. That was how we found out that on the first day of the war, Holland had fought back, kept the airfields around The Hague, and defended the city. But the Germans had made headway, mostly in the eastern part of the country. By the end of day two, the tide had started to turn. The Dutch had lost more ground. And by the end of day three, although The Hague was still safe, much of the country had been occupied by German forces. On day four, Queen Wilhelmina and other members of the royal family left for England on a British ship.

"Why would she go?" Bibi asked.

"Maybe she's Jewish," I suggested.

"No, *domoor*, she's not Jewish," said Peter. His voice cracked. "Not everyone who runs from the Nazis is Jewish. She must think the Germans will win. That's why she's establishing a government in exile."

"What's that?" I asked.

Peter sighed loudly. "Don't you know anything? It's a government that's run from a country other than its own."

"We'll be leaving soon, too," said Bibi.

"If we can."

"What do you mean?"

"It may not be easy to get out with all the fighting going on."

The following day, May 14, we went to school. Everyone was talking about the war and it was hard to concentrate on what the teacher was saying. Eventually, he gave up and asked us what we thought about what was happening.

"My father says we can still win, especially if the British help us," said Hetty confidently. Her father was in the military.

"Mine thinks we will give up soon," countered Bram, whose father was a doctor.

Susanne said, "My father says it's all but over now that the Queen is gone."

"The Germans don't want to harm us," Thijs cut in. "Like Hitler says, they just want to be closer to their enemy. England."

My head was pounding. I didn't want to hear any more. I just wanted to get away from them all. I got my wish. Just as Aart chimed in, Meneer Jansen, the principal, appeared at the door. He looked more tired than usual.

"You're being dismissed early," he said in a calm but serious voice. "Collect your coats and books and go directly home."

We all looked at one another. Why were we being sent home midday? Had the Germans returned?

"Now," he ordered.

Bibi was waiting for me by the front doors so we could walk together.

"Where's Peter?" I asked.

"He's run ahead," she said. As soon as we went outside she grabbed my arm hard. "Käfer!"

I looked in the direction she was pointing. A huge column of smoke rose high in the sky. A faint but steady booming sound came from the same place. And there was something else. A burning smell in the air.

I shivered.

"Let's go," she said. She took my hand, and we ran as fast as we could, arriving home just after Peter. In the front hall, Mama and Papa were waiting, dressed to go out.

"Papa, there's a smoke cloud in the sky," I said.

"The Germans are bombing Rotterdam. It's the beginning of the end. The Dutch will have to surrender now. We need to leave as soon as you change your clothes."

"Where are we going?"

"We'll cycle down to Scheveningen on the coast. I've arranged with a fisherman to take us to England."

Mama said, "Go and put your best outfit on over the clothes you're wearing, and your raincoat over that. Be quick. We need to leave now."

There was no mistaking the urgency in Mama's voice. We hurried and did as we were told. I grabbed my camera and Grandfather Avigdor's gold watch and stuffed them down deep in my trouser pocket. There was no room for Funny Bunny Blue. I gave him a farewell hug and placed him carefully on the bed. He'd been a good, loyal friend.

Then we got on our bicycles. Papa's had a basket of food strapped onto the back. Hidden in a false bottom was Mama's snuff box collection. We set off, Papa in the lead, Peter, Bibi, and me following. Mama brought up the rear. All the layers of clothing made it hard to cycle, but fear propelled me.

As Papa had drilled into us, we didn't say goodbye to anyone and we didn't look back.

"Goodbye, Thijs," I whispered so no one could hear. "Don't forget me."

The city was strangely quiet as we pedalled along, save for the distant din of bombs dropping on Rotterdam. Nearly everyone seemed to be indoors, probably listening to news reports on the radio. To the north, the sky was even darker than it had been when we'd left school less than an hour ago. Would there be anything left of Rotterdam?

We were on a side street in The Hague just halfway to Scheveningen when Peter's front tire went flat.

"*Vloek!*" he cried as his bike wobbled to a standstill.

We all stopped. There was no way to fix it quickly and no way Peter could ride with it flat.

"I can cycle home and get my repair kit," I offered, kicking myself for forgetting it.

"No," Papa said. "That will take too long. Peter can take your bicycle and you can ride on my handlebars."

Just then, a man on a bicycle came around the corner toward us. He was surprised—and not pleased—to see us. His short blonde hair looked like it hadn't been combed in days, and stubble covered his jaw. With no jacket, just a rumpled shirt, he looked like a ruffian. But his pants gave him away. They were unmistakably German army issue. My stomach lurched. I wondered if he was one of the paratroopers who'd been dropped into the city five days ago and disappeared. Maybe he'd been separated from his troop and been hiding ever since. I couldn't see a weapon on him, but perhaps he had one concealed.

He slowed down when he first spotted us, but then he tried to speed up and cycle around us. Papa, still straddling his bicycle, stepped in his path. The man braked, and Papa quickly seized his handlebars. The man tugged to the left, almost throwing Papa off balance. My heart was racing, but I moved my bicycle so I stood beside Papa, forming a barricade.

"Give me that bicycle," said Papa in German, his voice deadly calm.

"You can't have it," the man blustered, giving himself away by answering in German. He moved the handlebars sharply to try and dislodge Papa's hands. He wasn't successful. "It's mine."

"I think not." Papa was firm. "I think you've stolen it from one of my countrymen."

"What if I have? I own it now."

"I think you'll give it to me," said Papa, his voice rising. "If you don't, I'm going to start shouting at the top of my lungs that there's a German paratrooper in the street. And my family will join in. How long before you're surrounded by Dutch men eager to beat you up for invading their country?"

The paratrooper's hazel eyes narrowed. I could see that Papa had him. "And if I give you the bicycle?" he asked.

Papa shrugged his shoulders. The man handed it over reluctantly and, without a backward glance, quickly skulked off in the direction he'd been heading.

Papa looked at me. "That was brave what you did just then, Käfer." I didn't think Papa had noticed. It made me happy for a moment.

Peter climbed on to the paratrooper's bicycle and we set off again. Not five minutes later, I spotted two Dutch soldiers walking down a street to the right of us. I pointed them out to Papa.

"Look. We should tell them about the German!"

Papa nodded. "Good thinking, Käfer."

"I thought of it, too, Papa," said Peter.

"Käfer was the one who said something."

Peter looked crushed. He wasn't used to Papa finding favour with me. Papa told us to stay where we were, and he cycled down to the soldiers. They thanked him for the description and directions and asked where we were going.

"Scheveningen," Papa replied.

"Ah." They looked at Papa more closely, then over to the rest of us, sizing us up. "We've just come from there. Good luck."

As soon as we arrived in Scheveningen, I understood why the soldiers had wished us luck. Where the streets of The Hague were quiet, the outer harbour swarmed with people. They looked a lot like us. Whole families, smartly dressed. One woman wore a fur coat even though it was May. A child held a little dog in her arms. Some lugged heavy suitcases. Others had nothing but the clothes on their backs. They didn't take any notice of us. They were too busy offering money and jewels to fishermen to take them to England. But the fishermen were shaking their heads "no." It seemed no one wanted to set sail in the North Sea with a battle raging over Rotterdam. What about the fisherman Papa had hired? Would he be here?

"Rifat, what are we going to do?" asked Mama, her voice strained.

"Don't worry, Else," Papa said calmly. "Our boat is in the inner harbour, away from the crowd, and our captain will be waiting for us. It's all arranged."

Seeing Papa so unruffled calmed me. Everything would be all right. We followed him along the quay until he stopped in front of a small fishing vessel. It couldn't have been more than twenty-five metres long. This was going to take us across the North Sea? Papa called out. "Visser. We're here."

A muscular man with a pleasant face peeked out from the hold. He wore clogs, baggy pants, and a navy fisherman's sweater. A snug cap covered his head, but a few white blonde curls escaped from under it.

"You made it after all, Meneer Avigdor," he said as he climbed up onto the deck. He looked across the harbour at the increasingly vocal crowd, then over towards Rotterdam, where black smoke rose like a wall high above the city. He shook his head at Papa. "I was just about to go home. You're too late. I'm sorry. It's too dangerous to go out now with German planes over half the country. I'll only sail if my boat is requisitioned by the military."

A muscle in Papa's jaw twitched. "We must go now, Visser," he said quietly. But his voice had a dangerous undertone to it. "The Germans are busy bombing Rotterdam. This is the best time to get out."

Visser shrugged. He looked apologetic. "I can't help you."

"Please, Meneer Visser," Mama pleaded.

The captain glanced quickly at her, but he couldn't meet her eyes. He looked down at the deck.

"I've already paid you—and handsomely—to be fuelled up and ready to go," said Papa in the same quiet voice.

"I'll return your money," he said, reaching into his pocket.

"I don't think you understand, Visser. You're taking us to England. And we're going now." Papa reached into his pocket, but it wasn't money he pulled out. It was a handgun!

I stared disbelievingly at the gun, suddenly feeling light-headed. I didn't know Papa even owned a handgun, let alone knew how to use one. No wonder he hadn't been worried about the German paratrooper.

Papa pointed the gun at the captain, who looked more astonished than frightened. "You can't be serious!"

"I'm deadly serious," said Papa. "Holland will fall before day's end. We're not staying here to be persecuted by Hitler. We had enough of that in Germany. You and I had an agreement. I believe in honouring agreements. *I'm* requisitioning your boat." Papa paused and motioned to the boat. "I assume it's fuelled."

Slowly, Meneer Visser nodded his head. He still looked incredulous.

"Let's get going."

Papa instructed us to leave our bicycles on the quay and go onto the deck. Meneer Visser, realizing there was no choice, helped us down, one at a time, Papa's gun trained on him. Then he started the engine. It took several excruciating minutes before it warmed up and turned over and the rhythm became steady. I sat down on the deck. The boat bobbed under me. My earlier confidence had vanished. My stomach churned and my heart pounded. I just wanted to get away—from Holland and the crush of people that was growing bigger and louder on the quay across from us, oblivious to the little drama unfolding so close to them.

Instinctively, I got out my camera and focused on the scene. Even from a distance I could see the desperation written on every face. *Click. Click. Click.*

At last, we cast off. The captain steered the boat carefully out of the harbour. Papa stood beside him, his face inscrutable. I couldn't even imagine what he was thinking. I looked over my shoulder at the crowd. People were still frantically trying to convince fishermen to set sail. When they saw our boat leaving, they cried out. Some even started running towards where we'd been berthed, shouting for us to come back. But our boat was small. It would have been reckless to take any more passengers, and Meneer Visser was anything but foolhardy. What would happen to them, I wondered. Would they end up in a detention camp, like Aunt Charlotte? I turned away.

Before long we reached the open sea.

"We're heading for Folkestone, on the coast of England," Papa said, his voice steady.

"I know," replied Meneer Visser.

The calm water glimmered a deep blue-green. To the west, the sky was clear and the sun beat down. Despite the warmth, I shivered. I was still unnerved by what had happened. Mama hugged me close and kissed the top of my head. I breathed in her perfume and felt comforted. There wasn't another vessel in sight. No planes flew above in the sky. We were on our own. A small family in a little boat on a big, unpredictable sea. Behind us, in the distance, the sky was black with smoke. But I was safe. We were all safe.

At least for now.

I leaned back into Mama's arms and peeked up at her. Her eyes had a faraway look in them and a tear rolled down her cheek. I wondered if she was thinking about Aunt Charlotte. Would we ever see her again? I turned and hugged Mama as if I would never let her go.

Chapter 9

Papa remained vigilant beside Meneer Visser until we were well out to sea. Once he was convinced the captain wouldn't turn back, Papa grudgingly apologized for pulling a gun on him.

"I didn't know what else to do," he said simply.

Meneer Visser grunted then added fiercely, "Hitler is a liar." He looked over at the black sky above Rotterdam. "We Dutch will find ways to fight back. You'll see." He paused. "You were smart to get your family out. Hitler is determined to eliminate the Jews. I'm proud to help you."

I frowned. Did Meneer Visser think we were Jewish? Did we look Jewish? Or did he think we were because we were so determined to get away from Hitler?

I lay down on the deck and put my head in Mama's lap. I reached into my pocket and grasped Grandfather Avigdor's watch tightly in my hand. The combination of the warmth, the rocking of the boat, and Papa and the captain's voices lulled me to sleep. When I awoke, the sun hung much lower on the horizon. Peter, Bibi, and Mama stood at the stern looking out at the sea, though there wasn't anything really to see. Just water everywhere you turned. Papa and Meneer Visser talked quietly.

I reached for my camera. Looking through the viewfinder, I was struck by how confident they both looked. In different ways. *Click. Click.* Neither of them noticed. They were intent on their conversation.

I went over and stood beside Papa. He put his hand on my shoulder.

"I must say, Meneer Avigdor, so far it's an easier passage than I thought it would be. The North Sea can be very chancy. I wouldn't want to be crewing alone if it was rough. Let's hope it stays this way."

"What about when it gets dark?" Papa asked. "What will we need to look out for?"

"There will be no moon tonight, which is good for us in one way. We can sail unnoticed. Our big enemy is the weather, but the reports are for a calm sea. Our other worries are colliding with another boat or being hit by a U-boat or a floating mine we can't see in the dark—but there's not much we can do about any of those things." He shrugged.

Mines? Submarines? I felt my stomach knot up again.

"All we can do is pray that luck is on our side," Meneer Visser continued calmly. He looked right at Papa. "I have a feeling luck has always been on your side."

Papa's eyes didn't waver, but he smiled. "As a wise man once said, 'Luck is what happens when preparation meets opportunity.' I believe in being prepared."

They were silent for a moment. The engine chugged away.

"If all goes well, when should we reach Folkestone?" Papa asked.

"Four or four thirty, right around dawn. Here, take the wheel while I check the fuel tank. Just keep it steady."

Meneer Visser disappeared below deck. I took a deep breath and tried to quell my panic. "What will happen when we arrive in England?" I wanted to know.

"I don't know. I've never entered the country before on a fishing boat." He saw the worried expression on my face. "It will be fine."

Mama, who had overheard our conversation, joined us. She seemed to have recovered from her earlier grief. "Your papa is known at the British Air Ministry, Käfer," she said. "They want his new fuel pump."

"We still need to be careful what we say, Else." He looked at me. "You keep that to yourself, Käfer. All of it."

I nodded. But I was proud of Papa. He was clever. And fearless. I so wanted to be like him.

"Let's have some of those sandwiches you brought, Else. I'm sure Meneer Visser would appreciate something to eat as well."

After we ate, Papa suggested we try to sleep, so Mama, Peter, Bibi, and I huddled down on the deck under blankets Meneer Visser supplied. Before long, darkness fell. There was no moon, just stars, and the only sounds were the steady chugging of the engine and the water lapping up against the hull. The sea felt big and scary in the dark. Danger could be lurking anywhere. I shivered.

I was tired. I closed my eyes, but I couldn't sleep. My mind raced, playing the day over and over. The plume of smoke that became a wall over Rotterdam, turning the sky black. The desperate people gathered on the quay at Scheveningen, trying in vain to get passage out of Holland. Papa pulling a gun on Meneer Visser. And, when I'd exhausted those thoughts, there was the worry of what lay ahead. What would England bring? Where would we live? Go to school?

Eventually, I fell asleep, but it didn't bring any reprieve. In my dreams, somehow, I'd become separated from Mama and Papa. I saw them ahead in the distance. Mama turned to look for me, her face full of anguish, but even though I ran, I couldn't get to them.

Suddenly, a German shepherd blocked my path. A leash held it back, but its lips were curled in a snarl that exposed its sharp teeth. It lunged at me, over and over again, barking ferociously, slavering at the mouth. I eventually managed to get around it, but, by then, Mama and Papa were further away from me. I made my way toward them. I was gaining ground when a

Nazi solider confronted me, his gun trained on my chest. He yelled at me. I couldn't understand what he was saying, but his meaning was clear.

I turned and ran from him as fast as I could. He came after me. Gasping for breath, I raced around a corner. There was a doorway! I hid in it. The soldier ran past and disappeared from sight. By then, I couldn't see Mama and Papa at all and I was panicking. I had to find them, so I went back the way I'd come. Someone stepped in front of me. It was Hitler. I recognized his signature toothbrush moustache. He moved closer, pretending to be my friend, but I knew he meant to harm me. I looked around. There was nowhere to go. He advanced, hatred in his vivid blue eyes. I screamed at the top of my lungs—

Mama shook me awake. My heart pounded, and I was sweating. It had all seemed so real. "Shhh. Shhh, Käfer," she comforted me. "Everything is going to be all right. You've just had a nightmare."

"What's wrong with you?" Peter was angry at being woken up. "You're such a baby."

"Stop it," said Mama. Her tone was unusually sharp. "Can't you see your brother has had a bad dream? Be kind."

Peter opened his mouth to say something more, but at that moment, the engine stopped. The sudden silence was eerie. Meneer Visser swore. I sat up and looked around. The sun peeked over the horizon. There wasn't another boat in sight. And no shoreline.

Meneer Visser went to check the engine and reported that we had been leaking fuel without knowing it. Now the tank was empty.

He spoke calmly. I guessed that sea captains were used to the unexpected. He had on a bright yellow oilskin. He handed Papa one just like it.

"Here, put this on, Meneer Avigdor. Now, take the wheel and keep the boat pointed southwest. We can't be that far from land. With

83

any luck we'll encounter a friendly ship. I'm going to hoist a *nood vlag* so when we do see a boat, it will know we are asking for help."

Once the distress flag was up, the captain took the wheel again. For the next half-hour we drifted more or less in the right direction for the coast of England.

Finally, just as I'd started to think we were doomed to bob up and down on the waves forever, we spotted a ship on the horizon. My heart leapt. Meneer Visser looked through his binoculars then passed them to Papa. "It looks like a British destroyer to me, but it could be a German ship, posing as a British vessel."

A German ship? I took out my camera and looked through the lens to try to stay calm.

"It's hard to be certain from this distance. I'm thinking since it's so near to the coast it must be British," said Papa. "Can they not see us?"

"They can," said Meneer Visser. "Perhaps they don't trust us, even with our *nood vlag.* Let's try waving our arms."

Meneer Visser and Papa stood on the deck and vigorously waved. At first, nothing happened. Then, as we watched, a motor launch was lowered. Once in the water it started steaming over to our stranded boat.

When it was within earshot, the seaman in charge called out, "What's the problem?" He spoke in English and sounded friendly enough, but he had a rifle pointed at us.

"We were leaking fuel and ran out," Papa replied, also in English. He held his arms up to make it clear we intended no harm.

The launch's engine cut and the only sound was the water lapping up against the two boats. The seaman pointed to the Dutch flag, fluttering upside down, above our heads. "Where have you come from?"

"The Hague."

"Are you Dutch?"

Papa hesitated slightly. "Yes."

"Escaping from Holland?"

"Yes."

"Where are you bound?"

"Folkestone."

"That's where we're stationed. We're heading back there now. How many are you?"

"Just the captain, my family, and me. Six in total."

"You'd better come on board." The seaman lowered his rifle as the launch drifted alongside our boat. When it was close enough, Meneer Visser grabbed the gunwale. Another seaman took my hand and hoisted me onto the launch. Then he reached out to Mama and helped her on board. Bibi and Peter followed.

As he held out his hand to Papa, the seaman said, "You should know that Dutch forces surrendered to the Germans last evening."

Papa nodded grimly then glanced at Meneer Visser, who was lashing a rope to a metal ring on the launch.

The engine fired to life again and we headed for the destroyer.

And, from there, to England.

Part Three

England, May/June 1940

Chapter 10

When we arrived in Folkestone, full of sweet tea and biscuits courtesy of the crew, police officers met us. One took Meneer Visser away. We just had time to wave goodbye and call out our thanks. He wished us good luck with a cheery smile. Papa said the authorities would likely release him quickly and he would sail back to Holland.

The other officer introduced himself to Papa. They chatted briefly, then we accompanied him to a nearby building. The sign on the door read *Customs*. The officer asked Papa for our passports, which he took before directing us to a wooden bench where we were to wait. He disappeared into an office and we heard the soft murmur of voices coming from behind the closed door. A sign on the door read *Superintendent*. Another man, dressed in a suit and tie, stood behind the counter in front of us, but he paid us no attention. He concentrated on the papers in front of him.

We sat in a row. Papa, Mama, me, Bibi, and Peter. We were all tired. It had been a long day and night. I was relieved to have survived the bombing, the sea, the minefields, and the U-boats. The room was warm and stuffy. I leaned my head against the wall and was just starting to doze off when a confident-looking man emerged from the office. He had receding grey hair and steely blue eyes that matched the suit and waistcoat he wore. He put out his hand to Papa.

"Mr. Avigdor. My name is Christopher Hughes. Can you please come with me?" His voice was gruff but pleasant.

Papa stood and shook his hand. "I would like to bring my family as well."

Mr. Hughes tilted his head as if to object, but Papa spoke quickly and persuasively. "We had a frightening departure from

Holland, an exhausting trip across the North Sea, and now that we're here, it's all very strange, particularly for my children. I know you'll understand we need to be together."

"Of course." Mr. Hughes smiled briefly.

We followed him into his office where there were just enough seats for all of us. Peter, Bibi, and I wedged ourselves onto a small, uncomfortable sofa.

Mr. Hughes sat behind a wooden desk, Mama and Papa in chairs across from him. He took out a cigarette from a case and offered one to Papa, who declined, and then to Mama, who accepted.

"Thank you," said Mama as Mr. Hughes lit her cigarette. "A woman smoking in public. Just one of the many things forbidden in Hitler's Germany." Mr. Hughes shot Mama a quizzical look before sitting back in his chair. He directed his questions at Papa.

"According to the police officer who met you at the boat, you told him you are known to the British Air Ministry?"

Papa nodded. "Yes, I met with senior members of the ministry last November and again in January."

"And the purpose of the meetings?"

"I have patented a fuel pump the ministry is keenly interested in having mass produced. We discussed how that could happen as quickly as possible."

"You are an engineer by profession?"

Papa nodded again. "My field is aeronautics. I was director of the largest aeroplane parts manufacturing company in Berlin before leaving for Holland, where I established my own firm. We have been working with two companies here to manufacture gauges and fuel pumps for British fighters."

"If you have a successful company in Holland, why have you come to England?"

I could tell the question annoyed Papa, but he held his temper. He stroked his moustache before he answered in a measured tone.

"My wife and I are strongly anti-Nazi, Mr. Hughes. We suffered under Hitler in Germany, which is why we went to Holland. Five days ago, when the Nazis invaded Holland, we knew we had to leave. We have no desire to live under Hitler."

"But you *are* German?"

"If you have our passports, you know that we are. Were. Our rights as German citizens have been cancelled, so we are what is called 'stateless.'" Papa paused. "What you perhaps do not know is that I am on the Gestapo's hit list."

My heart thumped. Mr. Hughes' level gaze didn't waver. "Why is that?"

"Because I left Germany with the patent for my fuel pump, which is on the list of secret German weapons. I also have valuable information for the Allies on airplane and parts production."

"And what is your plan now that you're here?"

"To continue working with the British Air Ministry and companies I have a relationship with to ramp up production of the fuel pump."

"Hmmm." Mr. Hughes butted out his cigarette. "This is all very interesting, Mr. Avigdor, and I don't doubt that what you tell me is true. However, I cannot just take your word for it, as I'm sure you know. I need to verify your story and that could take some time. Unfortunately, as you are classed as an enemy alien, you will need to go to the Isle of Man within twenty-four hours. Your wife and children can remain here."

I gasped! The cigarette in Mama's hand trembled.

Papa frowned. "Is there no way that I can stay with them?"

Mr. Hughes shook his head. "I'm afraid not. They will be fine here in Folkestone. I assume you have some means?"

Papa nodded, but he didn't look happy. I could practically see the gears in his brain whirling, making arrangements.

"I recommend they stay at The Grand, then. It's on The Leas, Folkestone's promenade. It's not as fine as it was before the war—

many of the staff have been interned—but it's the best we have. I can take you there now and you can see your family settled in before you leave tomorrow morning. That should also give you some time to acquire a few more items of clothing and toiletries."

"How long will my husband be gone?" Mama asked, putting out her cigarette in the ashtray on Mr. Hughes' desk.

He shrugged his shoulders, but the look he gave her was not unkind. "I can't say. A few weeks, perhaps longer. In the meantime, Mrs. Avigdor, you and children are free to move about. I will return your passports once your status is determined." He smiled brightly. "Shall we go?"

The Grand Hotel lived up to its name. It was an imposing building perched on a cliff. Built of red brick, it had huge windows. On one side they overlooked the English Channel and the promenade; on the other, the hotel gardens.

I could tell that Mama was worried—I don't think she'd ever been away from Papa for more than a few nights—but I felt a shiver of excitement as we waited for Papa to check us in.

I'd never stayed in a hotel except for the time we were in Rome. But that was so long ago, I couldn't really remember it. And, anyway, it had just been for a few days. We could be at The Grand for weeks!

As I looked around, a boy about my age came in the front door. He gave us a curious look as he walked past on his way to the stairs. When he caught my eye, he smiled, revealing a crooked front tooth. He had a friendly, open face, framed with short, dark hair. *A possible friend*, I thought. Things were definitely looking up.

Our suite was on the second floor on the water side. There was a comfortable sitting room, a bathroom, and two bedrooms, one for Mama and Bibi, the other for Peter and me. Even having to share with Peter didn't dampen my spirits.

Although they were both tired, Mama and Papa decided to go into Folkestone and shop for clothes on the high street. Bibi elected to go with them. Peter and I said we would stay at the hotel.

"Make sure you watch out for Käfer," Mama said.

As soon as they left, Peter disappeared, muttering something about finding paper and a pencil so he could draw pictures of boats in the harbour. I grabbed my camera, put in a new roll of film, and set off to explore the hotel and grounds, hoping to find the boy I'd seen earlier.

I went downstairs to the lobby. I didn't encounter anyone on the way and the lobby was empty too, except for the clerk behind the front desk. He didn't even look up as I went by. He just kept drinking his tea and reading the newspaper. It felt like the hotel was half asleep.

I wandered out the front door and stood on the steps, gazing at The Leas across the way. It overlooked the harbour and the beach below and it was an impressive avenue, with wide drives and walkways, lush green lawns, and elaborate gardens and street lamps. There was even a bandstand. But, like the hotel, there weren't many people around. A few women walked arm in arm, a mother pushed a pram, and a couple of soldiers strode briskly by. I turned and walked around the building through the gardens to the back. And there, standing talking to a man wearing overalls and carrying pruning clippers, was the boy I'd seen earlier.

As I made my way towards the two of them, the boy caught sight of me. He waved and smiled. I smiled back.

"Hello," he said in Dutch.

"Hello," I replied back.

"Oh, good, you speak Dutch." He looked relieved. "I'm Tobias Katz, but my friends call me Toby. And this is Mr. Hall. He's the gardener. We've just met and we're trying to communicate, but without much success."

I smiled at Mr. Hall and said "Hello." Then I turned to Toby. "I'm Heinz. Heinz Avigdor. My friends call me Käfer."

"Where are you from?"

"The Hague. We came here on a fishing boat yesterday. We saw bombs fall on Rotterdam."

"I've never seen a bomb drop," Toby said. "I guess we were lucky to get out of Holland when we did."

"Where is your family?"

"My father has gone to the Isle of Man." Toby shrugged his shoulders. "We don't know why he had to go there. Probably something to do with our being Jewish. We don't know when he's coming back. My mother is upstairs resting. She's upset and misses him. My sister is keeping her company. Where is yours?"

"My parents have gone into Folkestone to buy clothes and my sister went with them. My brother is probably down at the harbour by now, drawing boats. My father is going to the Isle of Man tomorrow morning."

We looked at each other awkwardly. "What were you trying to say to Mr. Hall?" I asked.

"I wondered if there were bicycles at the hotel. I thought I'd go and explore. I can't stay inside a minute longer."

"That's a good idea!"

I turned to Mr. Hall. He had gone back to pruning a rose bush, so I tapped him on the shoulder. "Are there bicycles here?" I asked him carefully in English.

"There are," he smiled. "Come."

We followed him to the back of the hotel where several bicycles were leaning against the wall.

"You can use one of these. Just bring it back when you're done," he said.

Toby looked at me quizzically. "How do you know English?"

"I'm learning it at school. Papa says it's important to speak other languages. He speaks seven."

Toby's eyes widened with surprise, then he grinned impishly and cocked an eyebrow. "What do you think? Should we take a spin right now?"

I nodded enthusiastically, pushing aside Mama's warning to Peter to watch out for me. We each took a bicycle from the pile.

"Follow me!" said Toby. "I know the way to the harbour. We'll take the Zig Zag Path."

Off we went, Toby in the lead. I was so happy I'd learned to cycle before we left The Hague. I had no trouble keeping up with him. We rode along The Leas to a winding road that took us down to the harbour. Finally, a place that was busy! There were lots of ships docked, including the destroyer that had picked us up off the coast. I pointed it out to Toby. And there were soldiers and sailors everywhere. They all seemed very purposeful. No one paid any attention to us. I took a photograph of Toby on his bicycle with the ships in the background. *Click.*

There was something I wanted to ask him. "How do you know you're Jewish?"

He shrugged his shoulders, clearly puzzled by the question. "I don't know. I just am. My parents are Jewish. I'm to have my bar mitzvah when I'm thirteen. Why do you want to know?"

I sighed. "I think I may be Jewish."

He looked at me curiously. "You mean you don't know? Why do you think you are?"

"We left Germany and then Holland to get away from Hitler."

"Lots of people are doing that, Käfer. Not just Jews. He's an evil man."

"I know, but—" I couldn't explain to Toby the feeling that my parents were hiding something important about their past.

"Do you go to synagogue?" he asked.

I shook my head.

"Do you observe Shabbat?" He could tell I didn't know what that was. "Friday night dinner?"

Again, I shook my head.

"Then I don't think you are," he said.

Toby seemed satisfied I wasn't Jewish, but I still wasn't sure.

We watched the activity at the harbour for a little while longer, then I told Toby I needed to be back at the hotel when Mama and Papa arrived, and he said it would be tea time. As soon as he mentioned food, I realized how hungry I was. I hadn't had lunch.

We raced back up the cliff to The Grand. There was no sign of Mr. Hall, just his wheelbarrow and a rake leaning up against it. We put our bicycles back where we'd found them and agreed to meet the next morning after breakfast and explore some more. I knew I should be sad that Papa was going away, but, in truth, I was having too much fun to dwell on it.

I got back upstairs just in time. Mama, Papa, and Bibi arrived moments later, their hands full of shopping bags and boxes. They didn't notice I was flushed and breathing hard from the steep climb up the Zig Zag Path.

"What was Folkestone like?" Peter wanted to know as he tried on a shirt.

"Tiny," said Bibi. She was modelling a dress for Papa, who gave his approval with a smile. "At least the part we saw. And there weren't many trees or gardens. I was disappointed with the shops and you were too, weren't you, Mama?"

"It's certainly not Berlin or even The Hague," she agreed, looking at a new suit in the mirror.

"We did get some good watercolours and paper, though, so I can paint while we're here," said Bibi.

"Käfer, try these on," Mama said, pointing to a pair of grey flannel trousers lying on the sofa. "I want to be sure they'll fit. You seem to have grown practically overnight."

"Can you take my film in to be developed next time you go—"

"Look at the drawings I did while you were in town," interrupted Peter, showing Papa three pencil sketches. One was of a destroyer, the other two were battleships.

"Very nice work, Peter. Good detail."

"Were you down at the harbour?" Mama's voice was sharp. She was about to ask what I had been doing, but, luckily, at that moment she was distracted by a knock on the door.

It was a waiter with the tea Papa had ordered on the way in. There were scones with clotted cream and strawberry jam and a big pot of tea. I'd never had scones before, and they were surprisingly tasty, like sweet biscuits. I wolfed down three of them.

By then, we were all exhausted, so we went to our rooms to sleep.

At seven o'clock Mama came in and woke Peter and me up. "Get cleaned up and dressed quickly," she said. "Dinner service ends at seven thirty. Come down when you're ready and wear your new clothes. Papa, Bibi, and I are going now."

As we changed and brushed our hair, Peter asked, "Where were you this afternoon?"

"None of your business. Hurry up. We've got to go." I avoided his slap and raced out the door, slamming it behind me.

I scanned the dining room quickly as I entered. Like the rest of the hotel, it was quiet. Four soldiers occupied a table in the far corner. They were poring over papers and talking intently to one another. There were a few couples at other tables and not far from where Mama and Papa were sitting were Mrs. Katz, Toby, and his sister. Toby looked over and we grinned at one other conspiratorially.

"Look smart, you two," said Mama as we reached the table. Peter elbowed me and grabbed the chair next to Papa, but for some reason, it didn't bother me the way it normally did. Papa, as usual, didn't notice Peter vying for his attention.

"No menu tonight," he told us. "The waiter says it's fishcakes." He surveyed the room, stroking his moustache. He seemed calm

97

about being sent to the Isle of Man. "Don't expect too much. The English aren't noted for their cuisine."

Papa was right. The fishcakes were overcooked, and they came with boiled potatoes and tinned peas, but we were all so hungry, we gobbled it down. Partway through dinner I noticed Papa look up and smile at someone behind me. He got up from his chair. I turned. Standing by our table were Mrs. Katz, Toby, and his sister, who was a shy version of him. Peter and I stood up quickly.

"Good evening," said Papa, bowing slightly.

"Good evening," replied Mrs. Katz. "I thought as we seem to be the only 'foreigners' here, perhaps we should come over and introduce ourselves. I'm Miriam Katz. This is my son, Tobias, and my daughter, Ruth."

"Charmed," said Papa. "My name is Rifat Avigdor. This is my wife, Else, my daughter, Ellen, and my sons, Peter and Käfer."

"Where is Mr. Katz?" Mama asked with a smile.

"He's been taken to the Isle of Man." Mrs. Katz teared up slightly. "One day he's an esteemed physics professor at Utrecht University, the next, he's interned like a criminal." She shook her head in disbelief.

"Ah, I leave for there tomorrow morning," said Papa.

"I'm so sorry." Mrs. Katz paused. "Perhaps, Else, you and I could have tea tomorrow in the lounge, after breakfast."

"That would be lovely," said Mama. "I'll look forward to it."

"The children can get together at the same time," Mrs. Katz suggested. "I'm sure they can find something to amuse themselves."

Mama nodded in agreement.

"Until tomorrow, then."

We all went to bed early. Peter didn't stay awake long enough to say good night. I was really tired, but I was too wound up to sleep.

Eventually, I got up and felt my way into the sitting room. The curtains in all our rooms had been pulled tight for the blackout. Papa had explained the blackout—which included all the street lights, too—was so the Germans couldn't see Folkestone to drop bombs on it. I drew the curtains back so the moon could light the room.

Mama had made up a bed for Bibi on the sofa and she was curled up under a blanket. I crept over and sat down on the floor beside her.

"Bibi," I whispered. "Bibi. Are you awake?"

Her eyes popped open.

"Can't you sleep either, Käfer?" she whispered back.

"No. I can't stop thinking. So much has happened. How long do you think we'll be here?"

"Until Papa comes back, I suppose."

We were both silent as we contemplated life without Papa. It was impossible to imagine.

"We went to a telegram office and Mama sent a message to Frau Berkovitch," said Bibi. "Mama asked if she'd heard anything about Aunt Charlotte. Though how she would hear anything from London, I've no idea."

Silence again.

"I made a friend while you were in town," I said.

"Who? That boy, Tobias?"

"Yes. We borrowed bicycles from the hotel and went down to the harbour."

"What was it like?"

"Exciting! There were lots of military ships there and soldiers and sailors. I want to go back. I hope we get to go cycling again soon. And Toby says he'll show me how to fish if the hotel has any fishing rods."

"Do you think it's safe here?" Bibi's brow furrowed. I could hear the worry in her voice.

"I don't know," I replied. "We're not that far from Holland and Hitler is at war with the English. I'm not sure a blackout is enough to stop him."

"Let's try not to think about it." She yawned. "Tobias' sister looks nice. Maybe she'll be a new friend."

"I'm sure she will be, Bibi. You make friends wherever you go. Everybody likes you."

"Thanks, Käfer." Bibi yawned again. "I feel better just talking to you. I think I can sleep now. Can you? Will you stay with me?"

Bibi passed me one of her pillows and a blanket and I settled down on the floor beside her. She gave my hand a squeeze. Within minutes, we were both fast asleep.

Chapter 11

Right after breakfast the next morning, Mr. Hughes came to fetch Papa. We all stood outside the hotel and waved goodbye as they drove off. Mama got a little teary eyed then quickly pulled herself together.

"After a cup of tea with Mrs. Katz, I'm going to London," she announced. "I have some business to attend to. Peter and Bibi, you will stay here. You can amuse yourselves drawing and painting with the supplies I got you yesterday. I'm sure Mrs. Katz won't mind looking out for you. Käfer, you'll come with me. We'll take the train."

No bicycling or fishing with Toby! I was disappointed for a moment, but then I cheered up. An adventure with Mama was always fun and I was curious to see what London would be like.

Toby took the news well.

"I'll go bicycling by myself and find a good place to fish," he said good-naturedly. "Then I'll ask Mr. Hall if there are fishing rods we can use—I'll try sign language—and we'll go fishing tomorrow."

Mama and I took a taxi to the train station, where Mama bought our tickets. I thought she looked very stylish in her new navy and white polka-dot peplum dress with a matching little navy hat.

There weren't many people on the platform as I followed her into a carriage near the front and walked down a corridor to a compartment. Mama peered inside then opened the door. There were six seats, three on either side facing each other, all empty.

"You sit by the window there, Käfer. I'll sit across from you." It was as if Mama travelled by train in England all the time.

No sooner had we taken our seats than the train pulled out of the station. Before long, we were travelling through beautiful countryside. I sat quietly and gazed out the window at the patchwork of green fields bordered by hedgerows and dotted with farmhouses and barns. Every so often I spotted a church spire in the distance. At one point I saw what Mama said was a Roman viaduct. And the sky! It was a deep blue with large, puffy white clouds moving slowly across it. It was all so peaceful it was hard to believe that England was at war.

An hour after leaving Folkestone—the train now crowded with passengers, some of them soldiers—we rolled through the outskirts of London. Street after street of terraced houses gave way to larger buildings. And then we arrived at Victoria station. Trains sat steaming at platforms and crowds of people jostled each other. My pulse raced with excitement.

Mama stopped a uniformed conductor and asked him for directions, then started toward the exit. I followed her outside where we found a cab stand. Mama approached the first cab.

"65 New Bond Street, please," she said as we got into the back seat. Clearly, Mama had a destination in mind.

After a short drive, we pulled up in front of a red-brick building. The windows of a dress shop looked out at us. This must be where Mama was headed. As she paid the driver I looked up Bond Street. Stores selling all kinds of merchandise lined the street and a steady stream of motor cars and trucks—and big, red two-storey buses—clattered along it in both directions. A policeman at the corner directed traffic using a whistle and his hands. Along the sidewalk an elderly gentleman walked toward me leading a well-behaved wire-haired terrier on a leash. Behind him three young women carrying shopping bags laughed together. Two men in uniform overtook them and smiled back at them. The women laughed even more. Looking the other direction, I saw a newspaper vendor approach with a stack of papers under his arm. "Brussels falls to German forces," he called out. A driver motoring beside him honked his horn and narrowly missed hitting another motor car, while a man carrying a briefcase, oblivious to the near accident, stopped to buy a paper. I smiled with delight at the busyness of it all.

Mama glanced in the window of the dress shop for a moment, nodding her head in approval. But, surprisingly, she didn't go in. Instead, she opened the door next to the shop and went upstairs to the first floor. The sign on the door read Bentley & Co.

It was a jewellery shop, with long mahogany-and-glass counters. It smelled of old wood and beeswax and it was quiet after the noise of the street. We were the only customers. Across from us, a well-groomed man in a pinstriped suit stood on the other side of the counter. He was studying a diamond ring through what appeared to be a little magnifying glass held right up to his eye. He looked up when the door opened and smiled when he saw Mama.

"Good morning, Madame. May I help you?" he asked cheerfully, standing up straight.

"Is the owner here by chance? I know I should have made an appointment." Mama spoke surprisingly good English, I thought, but with an accent.

"Not a problem. He is here. May I tell him what it's about?"

"I have a Fabergé box he may be interested in buying."

"Ah, may I see it?"

Mama hesitated slightly then opened her purse and brought out a velvet bag with gold tassels. She put it on the counter and undid the cord, revealing the box. I recognized it immediately. It was the one Papa had given her after Peter was born. It was gold. Small and square, with sapphires, rubies, and diamonds attached along what looked like a vine climbing its way around three sides. It positively glowed against the royal blue of the bag.

The man's eyes widened appreciatively. He looked up at Mama. "I'll fetch Mr. Sheldon right away. Who shall I say is inquiring?"

"Mrs. Else Avigdor."

"Pleasure. I'll be back in a tick." He disappeared through a door behind the counter, taking the diamond ring with him.

As we waited, we walked slowly together along the counter, gazing at the jewellery, and pointing out pieces to one another that we particularly liked. It was a feast for the eyes. Rings and bracelets, necklaces and pendants—all made of gold and fabulous jewels. There was even a diamond tiara. Every piece was exquisite. But I thought none of them compared to Mama's Fabergé box.

I took Mama's hand and gave it a comforting squeeze. I knew she would be upset about parting with one of her treasured boxes. She squeezed mine back. "I'm glad you're here with me, Käfer. You're restful. Quite perfect company today." She kissed the top of my head. "Shall we do something fun when I've concluded my business?"

"Yes, please, Mama."

Just then, the gentleman returned. "Mr. Sheldon can see you now. Please follow me."

He led us to a small office just off the main display room. Another well-dressed gentleman, this one wearing a grey suit with a white handkerchief in the breast pocket, stepped forward, a smile on his face. The first man turned to Mama and said, "Perhaps you would prefer your son stay with me?"

Mama looked from him to me and back. "How thoughtful of you. Yes, that would be best."

While I waited for Mama, he showed me how to use his special magnifying glass, which he told me was called a loupe. He was just starting to explain what he looked for in the jewels when Mama returned. She looked wistful but not upset. I guessed she'd got a good price for the box, but I knew well enough not to ask.

"Come, Käfer. Let's go and have tea. I know just the place."

We walked a short way down New Bond Street and then along Brook Street. We stopped in front of a grand building.

"Here we are. Claridge's." Mama looked at her wristwatch. "And just in time for tea."

She took my hand and we swept past the doorman into the lobby. I gasped and stopped in awe. I'd never seen any place like it. It was so modern looking, with a soaring ceiling and a black-and-white marble floor laid out like a chessboard. The walls were a pale colour, but shiny, and the sconces were made of glass and chrome. Light poured in from a large, plain stained-glass window over the door. Beyond the lobby was a lounge, which looked similar in design, and that was where Mama headed.

"Do you like it?" Mama laughed.

"It's beautiful."

"The style is called Art Deco. There are places like this in Berlin, too, but this is a gem."

"Can I take a photograph of you, Mama?"

"Of course you can, Käfer."

She struck a pose like a fashion model. Which she could have been. *Click.*

"You're enjoying your camera, aren't you?"

"I want to be a photographer one day."

"Then perhaps you will be," she said. "I hope you can be whatever you want."

"Have you been here before, Mama?" I wanted to know.

"Yes, a few times. Once with Frau Berkovitch and once with Papa. They do a splendid tea."

And so they did.

We had finger sandwiches, scones with clotted cream and jam, and little pastries. Nearly every table was occupied with important-looking men—some of them in uniform—and elegantly dressed women. I couldn't help but see that Mama attracted a great deal of attention. Men looked at her admiringly; women, enviously. She noticed, but she didn't seem to mind.

"What do you think of London so far, Käfer?" she asked, taking out a cigarette and putting it in her ivory holder. A waiter leapt over to light it for her.

"I like it, Mama. It's exciting."

"It is, isn't it? There's so much to see and do here. It's unfortunate we have so little time today. But after tea, we'll go to Hyde Park before we take the train back to Folkestone. And perhaps we'll come to London another day. It depends on how long we're in England. I must bring Bibi in next to do some shopping."

I took a bite of my scone. "Are you sad about your Fabergé box, Mama?"

Mama looked at me thoughtfully. "I am," she said finally, "but I knew I might have to sell it one day, Käfer." She took another puff of her cigarette, put it out in the ashtray, and looked at me seriously. "It's important to have 'portable wealth.' Do you know what I mean?"

I shook my head.

"Small, but valuable things that you can take with you and sell if you need money quickly. That's one reason Papa buys me jewellery. Do you understand?"

I nodded. I knew Mama had just told me something significant.

"If we didn't own the boxes and the jewels, you and I wouldn't be having tea at Claridge's right now. Heaven knows where we'd be or what we'd be doing. Papa is a resourceful man, Käfer. Very few people have anything as valuable as that one little box." She thought for a moment. "And I still have another, if we ever need it."

The one Papa had given her when Bibi was born.

Mama read my mind. She reached over, tousled my hair, and looked me straight in the eye. "You are my darling boy, Käfer. Never forget that. I don't need a Fabergé box to remind me."

After tea, we walked to Hyde Park. We didn't go far into the park—Mama was anxious to get back to Folkestone and see Bibi and Peter—but we did walk through part of it. Large expanses of green grass and trees stretched out on either side of the wide walk. People sunned themselves in lawn chairs, girls skipped rope, and boys sailed model boats on the lake. We even saw a group of young women wearing khaki breeches, dark-green jumpers, and fawn-coloured, wide-brimmed hats, busy shearing sheep. Mama told me they were called Land Girls. A delighted crowd gathered around them. Mama asked about the sheep and one of the girls told her they were used to keep the grass short. I thought that was very clever!

My favourite part, though, was Speakers' Corner. Mama explained it was where anyone could stand up and talk on any subject. We heard several people spouting off, some about the war, others about religion. They all talked loudly so they could be heard above the hecklers, who were friendly for the most part.

"I don't think I'll ever do that," I told Mama, as I took a photograph of one particularly vocal man, who pointed his finger vigorously as he spoke.

"You don't have to, Käfer. No one does. The important thing is that you *could* if you wanted to. That's not possible in Germany or Holland or most of the rest of Europe now. Hitler doesn't approve of free speech. People who say things he doesn't like end up in detention camps. That's a big reason why Papa and I wanted to leave."

As Mama spoke, I suddenly recalled something that happened when I was with Aunt Charlotte at the Tiergarten. We were strolling along a path on our way to the Siegessäule, munching on fresh pretzels. The Victory Column—Golden Lizzy as Aunt Charlotte called it— was to be moved soon. It was part of Hitler's grand plan to turn Berlin into a "gleaming new capital," as Papa said, though it didn't sound like he thought that was a particularly good thing. Aunt Charlotte suggested we climb to the top to look over the city. We came across a small group of people gathered around a young man with dirty brown hair wearing a sweater vest and baggy trousers. We paused and watched him hand out leaflets as he talked passionately about communism. I didn't understand what he was saying, but Aunt Charlotte nodded her head in agreement. Others did too, though some argued against him. It was all well-mannered until, suddenly, four men in brown uniforms appeared. They wore peaked caps strapped under their chins and red-and-black swastika bands on their upper-left arms. They pushed their way roughly through the crowd and grabbed the young man, yelling at the rest of us to disperse. Aunt Charlotte started to protest then looked down at me. She took my hand and we walked away quickly. Just before we turned a corner, I looked back. Everyone had evaporated. It was as if nothing had ever happened.

I opened my mouth to tell Mama about it, but she looked so happy listening to the speakers, I didn't want to spoil it for her.

We arrived back in Folkestone late in the afternoon. As we walked across the hotel lobby, the front desk clerk called to Mama. He held a buff-coloured envelope in one hand.

"Mrs. Avigdor. A telegram arrived for you earlier."

Mama turned pale and swallowed hard. She walked slowly over to the desk and took it from the clerk. She didn't look at it right away. Instead, she headed for our rooms, her step heavy.

"What is it, Mama?" I asked. She didn't answer.

Once inside, she sank into a chair in the sitting room, took a deep breath, opened the envelope, and read the telegram.

"Oh, no." She dropped it on the floor. The expression on her face was so sad.

I picked it up and read it.

CONFIRMED LOTTE TRANSPORTED TO DACHAU CONCENTRATION CAMP. COME AND SEE ME IN LONDON. MARGARETHE

Chapter 12

Eventually, Mama told me to go to dinner with Bibi and Peter. She gave me an absent-minded hug, retreated to her room, and closed the door.

I found them in the dining room with the Katzes. Everyone had just ordered. I sat down. I didn't feel like eating, but I pretended everything was all right. I didn't want to say anything about the telegram in front of the Katzes.

"Where is your mama?" asked Mrs. Katz.

"She's tired. She's gone to bed. She said she'd see you tomorrow."

"Well, you did have a busy day. Did you enjoy London?"

"Yes."

"You sound a bit weary too, Käfer. You're probably hungry. It's roast beef tonight. The waiter says it's very good."

It was tough—did the English overcook everything?—but I didn't care. I had no appetite. I just picked at my meal, anxious to finish it and talk to Bibi and Peter alone. I did my best to seem normal as I talked about my day. I left out the part about selling the Fabergé box—I was pretty sure Mama wouldn't want Mrs. Katz to know about that—but I told them about tea at Claridge's and Hyde Park.

"I don't know why Mama took you," Peter said peevishly.

But Bibi smiled, delighted I'd had a good day. "You'll have to see what Ruth and I painted while you were away, Käfer."

"I'd like that. I'm sure your paintings are both very good."

"B-b-b-b-Bibi's is m-m-much b-b-b-better than m-m-m-m-mine," said Ruth softly. She was a bit shy, but she had a lovely smile and it was clear she and Bibi had become fast friends.

"But I've been painting much longer than you have! You have talent, Ruth. You just need practice."

"Mr. Hall has given me two fishing rods and some bait," Toby chimed in. "We can go tomorrow, Käfer. The best time to catch something is early morning or late afternoon."

"How early in the morning?" I wanted to know. I was thinking we could go and come back before Mama even noticed me missing.

"How about five o'clock? The sun should be rising. Best time for the fish to bite."

"I'll meet you in the lobby."

Once dinner was over, Bibi, Peter, and I went upstairs. The door to Mama and Bibi's room was still closed. I told them about the telegram and how Mama had reacted.

"What will happen to Aunt Charlotte?" Bibi asked.

We both looked at Peter. He was clearly torn between showing he knew more than we did and upsetting us more.

"I don't know anything for certain. Just what Ernst told me."

I wasn't sure I wanted to hear. But I didn't move. Neither did Bibi.

Peter took a deep breath. "They make people in the camps do hard labour and beat them if they don't work fast enough. They starve them and make them sleep on hard bunks, packed in so tight they have to lie on their sides, like sardines in a tin."

Bibi and I gasped.

"That's cruel," Bibi cried.

"Maybe the place where Aunt Charlotte is isn't as bad as that." I suggested, really wanting to believe it. "They probably treat women better than men."

Peter looked doubtful, but he didn't argue.

"Do people ever get out of the camps?" I asked.

111

"Not very often. Sometimes, though. That's how Ernst's father knows about what goes on. Ernst has an uncle in Germany who was in a camp and told him all about it."

"Did he escape, or did they let him go?"

"They let him go. If you try to escape, you may be shot."

We were silent for a long while as we tried to imagine Aunt Charlotte in such a place.

"We need to watch out for Mama and try to cheer her up," Bibi said eventually.

"How will we do that?" I wanted to know.

"I'll show her my painting and ask her to choose a subject for my next one. And she can come sketching with Ruth and me."

"I can take her for a long walk along The Leas and down to the harbour," Peter offered.

I couldn't think of anything I could do to make Mama feel better. Bibi read my mind.

"If you catch a fish tomorrow, Käfer, you can get the chef to cook it especially for Mama. She'd like that."

I put Grandfather Avigdor's watch on my bedside table as I always did, but I was so worried I wouldn't wake up in time that I didn't sleep very well. I was also upset about Aunt Charlotte. And Mama.

At last it was five o'clock. I dressed quickly, let myself out of the suite quietly without waking Peter, and ran downstairs to the lobby. Toby was already there. In his hands were a can of worms and two fishing rods with hooks already tied on them.

We got the bicycles and started off. The sun was just peeking over the horizon. It was a thrill to be out so early! And on our own. The ride took longer than our first trip by far, but Toby had done his homework well. From the cliff where we stopped we could see the beach and the pier below, and both were deserted. To top it off, it was a beautiful, clear summer morning. I inhaled the fresh sea air. This was going to be fun.

"Let's leave our bicycles here," Toby suggested.

"Good idea." I agreed. They would be safe. There wasn't anyone else around.

But just as we were ready to start down the cliff to the pier, I spotted two small dinghies in the water, each with two men in them. Even at a distance, there was something about the men that looked odd. The only people who would be out this early would be fishermen, but they weren't dressed like fishermen and they had no rods or nets.

I grabbed Toby by the arm and pointed at them. As we watched, I saw something further out in the water. I knew what it was immediately. I dropped to the ground, pulling Toby with me. The grasses covered us.

"There's something strange going on," I whispered.

Toby looked at me quizzically.

"That's a U-boat going down." I pointed.

Toby's eyes widened. "How do you know?"

"Peter made a model of one for his friend Ernst. It must have dropped them off."

We crawled down as quietly as possible until we were almost where the grass met the beach. By this time, the four men had landed and brought their dinghies onto the sand. We stayed still. Keeping our heads down as best we could, we watched them through the grass.

They started letting the air out of the dinghies. They worked quickly and silently, concentrating on the task at hand, but, finally, one of them spoke. In German. I could hear clearly because his voice carried in the wind which blew towards us.

"Was passiert als nachstes?" What happens next?

"Speak English," snapped another. His English sounded flawless. He was older and seemed to be in command. "We'll hide the dinghies here. By the time anyone finds them, we'll have blended into the countryside. I've got some British pounds for each of you, a map of the area, and a list of names and addresses of people who can help if you get into trouble."

"I don't like the idea of living rough," grumbled one of the others, with a scowl on his face. "I don't see why we can't stay at inns."

"Because it may raise suspicions," said the one in charge. He took a revolver from the pocket of his trousers and put it down beside him. "We're not on a holiday. We're here to blend in with the locals and get information for the Führer."

I looked at Toby in horror. He couldn't understand what they were saying, but I knew without a doubt that they were spies. With contacts in the area. Once they went their separate ways, it would be hard to find them. And they weren't going to stay long at the beach. I had to do something! My heart was pounding, and I knew Toby's was too. I signalled to him to stay and watch the direction they went when they left. I started to crawl back as quickly as I could to where our bicycles were. It seemed to take forever, but I knew I had to be careful. If they discovered us, there was no telling what they would do.

I didn't notice the piece of glass hidden in the grass. I cried out as I scraped my arm on it.

"What's that?" asked the complainer sharply. I froze. I kept my head down and held my breath.

At that moment, a bird of prey that had been circling overhead plummeted to earth no more than ten feet in front of me; then it rose almost as quickly, a small creature, mewing loudly, caught in its talons.

"You're just edgy," said the one in command as he watched the bird fly off. "Let's finish deflating these dinghies and get out of here before someone spots us. I'm hungry."

114

Finally, I made it to the top of the cliff and, bicycle in hand, looked for a visual marker. I couldn't find one, so I took out my handkerchief and tied it to the branch of a nearby tree. Satisfied that I could get back to the exact spot, I pedalled as fast as I could towards Folkestone. My legs and lungs burned.

I'd been cycling for about ten minutes when I saw a military truck speeding toward me. I braked quickly, hopped off my bicycle, dropped it on the ground, and started waving my arms. The truck came to a halt. Four soldiers sat inside. I was relieved to see that all of them had guns.

"What's wrong?" the driver asked, leaning out the window. He had dark hair parted on one side and a small, dark moustache. He took a drag on his cigarette before tossing it to the ground.

"Spies. On the beach." I was breathless.

They glanced at one another. I could see they were skeptical.

"It's true," I gasped. "I'm Dutch, but I speak German. They were talking in German. And English. Gathering intelligence. That's what they said. Dropped off by a U-boat. I saw it. Hurry. They won't stay long."

"It's possible, I suppose," said one of the soldiers in the rear. "It would be smart to drop off spies who spoke English and could blend in with the locals."

"That's the phrase one of the spies used!" I said excitedly.

"If the lad is right, we'll be doing an important thing," said the one sitting beside the driver. "If he's not, no harm done."

The driver turned to me. "Leave your bicycle here by the side of the road and get in. You can take us to where you last saw these German 'spies.'"

He put the pedal down to the floorboard. As we raced along, I kept my eyes peeled for the tree and the handkerchief I'd tied to the branch. Finally, I saw it fluttering in the breeze.

"There," I said. I pointed to it. The driver braked hard but overshot it and had to reverse the vehicle.

"Good idea. You're a clever young man. Now where to?"

I led them silently across the cliff. Just before the edge, I dropped to one knee. I signalled them to do the same. The four Germans were still there, but they were getting ready to leave. Down to the right, I thought I could make out Toby lying in the grass.

I wondered what the soldiers would do.

"Let's wait here," said the driver quietly. "They'll have to come up to the road. We'll approach them then."

Sure enough, soon the Germans climbed up the cliff. We all moved back, out of sight. "One of them has a revolver," I whispered. At that, the driver told me to go back to the road where I would be safe. I walked slowly backwards. I wanted to see what would happen.

When the Germans reached the top, the driver silently stood and came up behind them. He signalled to the other three, who ran to surround the Germans, guns drawn. I peeked from behind a tree.

"What have we here?" asked the driver.

"We're refugees from Holland," said the German in command. Now he spoke in broken English.

The driver looked at the others and raised an eyebrow. "Let's see your identification papers."

He shrugged. "We have no papers."

"What have you got in those knapsacks? Empty them."

The Germans glanced at one another nervously. Reluctantly, they opened them.

The driver and the soldier from the back seat moved in to take a closer look, while the other two kept their guns trained on the

Germans. "Just clothes?" They turned the knapsacks upside down and emptied them. Out fell wireless radio transmitters and receivers.

"What do refugees need with these? Search them," the driver ordered.

It didn't take long for the British soldiers to find the revolver. That sealed the Germans' fate.

"You're coming with us," the driver told them.

While one soldier gathered everything up, the other two handcuffed the spies and marched them to the truck.

"You were supposed to go back to the road," said the driver when he saw me.

I shrugged and grinned at him.

He shook his head affably. "Did you see how they got here?" he asked.

I nodded. "In two inflatable dinghies. They're hidden in the grass. I'm sure my friend Toby will be able to show you."

"You're not here alone?"

"My friend is hiding down on the beach. He bicycled with me. We were going fishing."

"Is he still there?"

I nodded. "He's lying in the grass."

"What's your name, young man?"

"Käfer," I replied, careful to use my nickname. Papa had cautioned me that Heinz was too German for England.

"What kind of name is that?"

"Dutch, sir."

"Where do you live?"

"I don't have a home right now, sir. My parents, brother, sister, and I came here from Holland a few days ago. We're staying at The Grand."

"Make a note of that," he said to one of the others. "Can you and your friend get back to where you left your bicycle?"

"Yes, sir."

"You may have done a very good thing, here, Käfer. But don't say a word about it to anyone." His dark brown eyes bored into mine. "There will be hell to pay if you do."

"I won't," I promised.

I ran down to where Toby was hiding, almost falling a couple of times. He looked relieved to see me.

As we hiked back up the cliff, I told him what had happened.

"That was quick thinking, Käfer. And really lucky that you speak English so well. You might not have convinced the soldiers otherwise." He gave me a friendly elbow in my side.

"You were brave, too, Toby. Those spies could have stumbled on you. And maybe hurt you."

Up at the top of the cliff, the Germans sat on the ground. They looked dejected. The British soldiers smoked cigarettes and waited for another truck to arrive to pick up the prisoners. Toby pointed out where the dinghies were hidden, before they bade us a cheery farewell and cautioned us again to keep our mouths shut. Toby and I cycled back slowly—me sitting on the handlebars—until we found my bicycle, still lying by the side of the road. We couldn't stop talking.

"I was scared when you left," Toby said. "What if they saw me?"

"I was frightened too. I've never cycled that hard in my life. Boy, was I relieved to see those soldiers."

"What do you think will happen to the spies?" Toby asked.

I thought about Aunt Charlotte. She'd spied for the British from what Papa had said, and the Germans had sent her to a concentration camp. I shivered.

"I don't know," I said. "But it won't be good."

For the rest of the day we were bursting to tell someone about our adventure, but we didn't, mindful of the warning we'd been given. We stayed at the hotel. Mr. Hall produced a croquet set and he showed us all how to play. Mama and Mrs. Katz watched. Mama even smiled a few times at our antics, though her smile never reached her eyes, which were rimmed with red.

As we made our way back to the suite, Bibi asked if I'd caught anything.

"Oh!" I started to say, the secret bubbling up, but I caught myself in time. I shook my head. "The fish weren't biting."

Chapter 13

The next morning, after breakfast, as Mama, Peter, Bibi, and I left The Grand to walk along The Leas, a motor car pulled up and Mr. Hughes got out. I felt Mama tense when she recognized him. I moved closer to her and took her arm, giving it what I hoped was a reassuring squeeze.

He strode over and tipped his hat to her. "Good morning, Mrs. Avigdor."

"Mr. Hughes. Is there something wrong? Is my husband all right?"

"As far as I know, he's fine, Mrs. Avigdor. I'm not here about your husband. I'm here about your son." He looked over at me.

Mama pursed her lips. "What has Käfer done?"

"Nothing bad. Perhaps I could speak to you and him alone." He looked pointedly at Peter and Bibi.

Mama hesitated then told them to go on ahead.

"Now, what is this about?"

"It seems your Heinz is something of a hero."

"Käfer?" She looked at me then back at Mr. Hughes. "What do you mean?" Mama was obviously mystified.

Mr. Hughes told Mama what had happened the day before. "The four men are now in custody being questioned. And it's all thanks to young Heinz."

Mama looked at me with surprise. "Well done, Käfer."

I think both she and Mr. Hughes would have said more, but just then, a shiny black motor car pulled up. The driver, who wore a British army uniform, got out smartly. Another man, dressed in civilian clothes, climbed out equally fast from the passenger seat. He was tall and wiry, with piercing eyes, and he looked closely at us as the soldier opened the back door. A portly gentleman, cigar in hand, emerged. He wore a dark suit and a navy blue–and–white polka-dot bow tie. On his head was a bowler hat, and in his right hand he held a walking stick. He wasn't a tall man, but he had a commanding presence.

"What's going on here?" he practically barked out in what Mama called a posh accent. "Who are you?" He directed this at Mr. Hughes.

"Christopher Hughes, Customs, at your service, sir." Mr. Hughes was clearly awestruck. So were people walking along the promenade. Everyone had stopped to stare in our direction, whispering among themselves. I turned back and looked right at the man with the bow tie. He must be someone important, but who?

"What are you doing here?" he asked Mr. Hughes.

"I came to commend this young man on his quick thinking and—"

"What did he do?"

Mr. Hughes coughed. "He helped us capture four German spies." He spoke softly.

"Did he?" The gentleman turned his attention to me. "What's your name, young man?"

"Käfer Avigdor."

"Harrumph. Unusual name. And this is your mother?"

"Yes, sir."

The gentleman bowed to Mama before turning back to me. "Where is your father?"

"He's on the Isle of Man, sir." I added, "I don't know why."

"You're not English. Where are you from?"

"Holland, sir."

"And what did your father do there?"

"My father is an aeronautical engineer," I said proudly. "He's invented many parts for aeroplanes. Now the British Air Ministry wants his fuel pump."

"Käfer," Mama said warningly. "We're not to talk about that."

"No, no, it's all right," said the gentleman, glancing at Mama. "He can tell me. What is it about this fuel pump that's so special? Do you know, Käfer?"

"It lets fighter planes go up and down quickly without stalling."

"Really? That *is* an important advance. Do you want to be an aeronautical engineer like your father?"

I hesitated. "No, sir, I'm not clever like he is."

"Humph. You were clever enough to recognize people who were up to no good." He gave me a pat on the back. "Now, you must promise me something." He leaned over and stared hard into my eyes. He didn't blink. "You must *not* tell anyone what you did. Do you understand? *No one*. It's a secret."

I gulped and nodded at him. He turned and focused his pale blue eyes on Mama with the same concentration.

"You'll see to it, Mrs. Avigdor?"

Mama nodded.

He seemed satisfied.

"Good luck, young man," he said, tipping his hat and heading for the front door of the hotel. "I think you'll go far in this world. Keep your eyes and ears open. You never know what you might uncover. Find General Brook, Murray," he said, addressing his driver.

"What an extraordinary man," said Mama slowly, still looking at the now-empty front door of the hotel. "And what a strange encounter." She shook her head as if to remove the memory. "I'm very proud of you, Käfer. Evidently, you showed real courage and initiative. But we won't speak of it again."

We never did.

Chapter 14

Three days later, much sooner than we expected, Papa returned from the Isle of Man.

That afternoon we were all out in the hotel garden. Mama and Papa lounged on striped canvas deck chairs. They held hands and couldn't stop smiling at one another. Peter sat on the grass beside Papa, and Bibi and I lay on our backs, watching the clouds go by.

"There's one that looks like Funny Bunny Blue," said Bibi, pointing to a cloud shaped like a rabbit.

"It does," I agreed. "I wonder what it will turn into next."

"Do you miss Funny Bunny Blue, Käfer?" Mama asked lazily.

"A little, but I'm too old now to take a stuffed animal to bed."

A shadow passed over me. I looked up into the sun. The hotel manager stood over me, but he looked at Papa.

"Mr. Avigdor. Have I said how pleased we are to have you back?"

Papa nodded. "Thank you."

"You will have noticed that we are getting busier."

Although Papa had been back only for a few hours, he couldn't have missed the changes at The Grand. Over the past few days, it had gone from sleepy to bustling. A real hive of activity. Military personnel had been arriving and had taken over the rooms at the other end of the corridor from us. Boxes had been delivered and unpacked. Peter said it looked like radio equipment.

"Yes, and I believe you may even have had a visit from Mr. Churchill, your new prime minister?" suggested Papa.

The manager coughed. "I wouldn't care to comment on that, sir.

But I have been informed that the Royal Air Force is going to require the entire hotel. Almost immediately." He looked uncomfortable.

"That isn't a problem," said Papa, stroking his moustache. "We'll leave tomorrow. I'm assuming that will be soon enough? I'll come and settle the bill after we've had our tea."

"Very good, sir. I'll send it out directly. And may I say what a pleasure it has been to serve you and your family." He paused, as if debating whether or not to say something else. "Probably for the best, sir, to be moving on. I have it on good authority that a mass evacuation of Folkestone is imminent as we find ourselves increasingly in the eye of the storm."

"What does he mean?" asked Bibi, as soon as he had left.

"The east coast of England is preparing for a possible invasion by the Germans," explained Papa. "It's not going to be safe here much longer."

"Where are we going now?" I asked.

"First, London. You, your brother, sister, and Mama will stay for ten days before setting sail for Canada. I'll remain another week to conclude some business with the Air Ministry, then I'll take another ship and join you."

"Canada!" said Bibi. "That's all the way across the Atlantic Ocean, Papa."

"I thought you were setting up your business here, Papa. How long will we stay in Canada?" Peter asked.

"For a long time," said Mama. "It's a new country for a new life. Just what we need."

We were all silent for a few moments, taking in the news.

"Will we go across the ocean on a big ship, Papa?" Bibi asked.

"Yes, Schatzi, a very big ship. An ocean liner."

That sounded safer than a fishing boat to me. "Where will we stay while we're in London, Papa?" I asked.

"At Claridge's. I understand you've had tea there, Käfer. This visit you'll have a chance to see a little more of the city." There was no mistaking the excitement in Papa's voice. I was excited too. I had loved the hustle and bustle of London. And the prospect of taking an ocean liner across the sea made me tingle all over.

The following morning, we checked out. I hated to say goodbye to Toby, Ruth, and Mrs. Katz, who still had no idea when Mr. Katz was coming back. Ruth and Bibi hugged.

"Take my watercolours and brushes," said Bibi, handing them to Ruth. "Papa said he would get me some in London. You're much better than you think you are, so keep painting, and when you do, think of me!"

"I w-w-will. You've in-in-inspired me." Ruth blinked back tears and so did Bibi. In the few days she and Bibi had palled around, her stammer had improved noticeably and she chewed on her fingernails far less.

Toby and I shook hands.

"I'll miss you, Käfer."

"I'll miss you, too, and I'll never forget you." I meant it. Toby and I had known each other only a short time, but we had shared an incredible adventure, one that we had to keep secret.

"Let me take a photograph of all of you." I posed the Katzes with The Grand behind them and snapped the picture. *Click.* They were leaving later in the day for Croydon, where they would wait for Mr. Katz to return from the Isle of Man.

Then we got in the cab, and the Katzes gathered around to wave goodbye. Just as the driver pulled away from the hotel, Peter suddenly cried out, "My drawings! I forgot them. Can we go back?"

"No," said Papa.

Peter's face fell. "But I worked so hard on them."

"We don't want to risk missing the train. You can draw others."

Claridge's was every bit as splendid as I remembered. This time it was Bibi who stopped in her tracks, gasping as we entered the lobby. I laughed and pulled her forward toward the front desk where Papa was checking in.

The desk clerk peered at Papa's registration card. He frowned.

"The Grand Hotel, Folkestone. When did you leave there?" He looked up at Papa.

"This morning," said Papa. "Why do you ask?"

"It was badly shelled not more than an hour ago!"

Shelled! It must have happened right after we left. My excitement evaporated, and my heart started to pound. What about Toby? Was he safe? And Ruth? And Mrs. Katz?

"We would have been there if we'd gone back for Peter's drawing," said Bibi slowly. We looked at one another in horror.

"Was anyone hurt?" Papa asked the desk clerk.

He shook his head. "It was a miracle. The soldiers were on church parade at the time."

"What about the other residents? Are they safe? We have some friends staying there."

"I don't know, sir, but I can telephone and see if anyone knows. What are their names?"

"Katz. Miriam, Ruth, and Toby. Please let me know as soon as you find out anything."

The next hour passed by slowly as we waited for word. I fidgeted with a throw pillow, feeling on edge. It didn't seem possible that the Katzes could be dead. They had been so alive such a short time earlier.

Finally, the manager knocked on our room door. I held my breath.

But he was smiling in the doorway. "Your friends are safe. They were watching the parade when the shell hit."

After that, the week went by in a blur. Mama was determined we would all be properly kitted out for our voyage, so we spent a lot of time in clothing stores. Papa spent the days in one meeting after another.

But one morning shortly before we left for Liverpool, he announced that he would take Peter and me to a cricket match that afternoon.

"What's cricket?" I wanted to know.

"It's a very popular game, especially in Commonwealth countries, like England, Australia, India, and Canada," said Papa. "We're going to see London Counties play British Empire at Lord's Cricket Ground."

Although much of Lord's had been taken over by the Royal Air Force, the playing area, pavilion, and stands were still being used for cricket. That was because cricket kept people's morale high, said Papa.

The stands were filling up when we arrived. Everyone seemed to have a favourite team, or club. Papa suggested Peter and I pick one and cheer for it to make it more fun. I chose London Counties; Peter, British Empire.

"What do you think, Peter?" Papa asked as London Counties got another run.

"It's very interesting, Papa."

"And, you, Käfer. Are you enjoying it?"

"It's fun to watch, Papa, but I don't really understand how it's played."

"You'll learn," he said. "You'll be playing cricket at your new school in Toronto."

"What's Toronto like, Papa?" I asked.

"I don't know. I've never been there. All I know is that I will be able to set up my business quickly and start supplying the

Allies with fuel pumps." He paused. "And it's far from the battlefields of Europe."

London Counties scored again, to the delight of about half the crowd. When the cheers subsided, Papa spoke again.

"I want you to listen carefully. When we arrive in Canada we will put the past behind us. We will look forward only. To the future. And we will be Canadian. Not German. Not Dutch. Do you understand me?"

We both nodded.

"Won't we ever come back to Europe?" Peter asked. I knew he really wanted to stay in London. I did, too. But Papa's mind was made up.

"One day, when the war is over, to visit, perhaps," said Papa. "But our new home will be Toronto. There's a world globe at the hotel. Tonight, I'll show you exactly where we're going."

After that, I found it even harder to concentrate on the game. I kept thinking about Toronto and what it would be like. Later, I found out that London Counties won the match, but we were long gone by the end because the game took two days to play!

As we left the stadium, newspaper sandwich board signs announced, "Belgium Surrenders."

"We're not leaving a moment too soon," Papa observed as we walked past them.

A few days later, we took the train to Liverpool to board the *SS Somerville*, bound for Canada and our new life. Papa took me aside before I walked up the ramp to the deck. He had to raise his voice to be heard over the din. The Liverpool docks were enormous. And chaotic. All around us soldiers, sailors, and airmen from Britain, Australia, New Zealand, and Canada were arriving and leaving, cargo was being loaded and unloaded, and passengers like us were trying to stay out of the way.

"You take care of Mama and Bibi on this voyage, Käfer," he said, putting his hand on my shoulder.

"Me?"

"Yes, you. I'm very impressed by how brave and resourceful you can be."

That was the closest Papa ever came come to acknowledging that he knew the role I'd played in helping to capture four German spies—and how that had likely gained his early release from the Isle of Man.

It made me brave. "Papa, are we Jewish?" I ventured.

He looked at me seriously. "You remember what I told you at Lord's, Käfer? We are very fortunate that Canada will take us in. We will be Canadian. That's all that matters."

I nodded. "I'm sorry I'm a disappointment in some ways," I said softly.

Papa looked puzzled.

I shrugged. "You told Herr Berkovitch that Peter would follow in your footsteps, but I wouldn't because I don't have the mind of an engineer."

Papa's eyes widened, and he stared at me for a long moment. "It's true you don't have a talent for engineering, but you are clever in other ways, Käfer. And you'll be successful at whatever you put your mind to—as long as you work hard at it. This I know for a fact."

"Yes, Papa." I smiled at him and he smiled back.

We waved goodbye from the deck until Papa was just a speck on the quay. Then I took Mama's arm. We turned our backs to Europe and faced the new world, with the sun shining on our faces.

The End

Author's Note

Käfer (right) and his brother and sister

While *Boy from Berlin* is a work of fiction, it is based on historical facts.

In 1938, Käfer and his family lived in Charlottenburg, an affluent neighbourhood in Berlin. His father, Rifat, was a successful aeronautical engineer originally from Constantinople; he was the director of Deutsche Benzinuhren-Gesellschaft, one of the country's largest aeroplane parts firms. Rifat invented and patented a self-priming fuel pump that was on the list of the Third Reich's secret weapons. It was used in both Spitfire and Messerschmitt bombers by the end of the Second World War. While living in Holland, he also worked with the British Air Ministry and provided information about German aircraft and parts development and production.

Rifat was a Sephardic Jew. Else was a German Jew. They lived a privileged life in Berlin in the 1910s and 1920s. But, being Jewish and anti-Nazi, they suffered when Hitler rose to power. Like many Jewish parents at that time, they shielded their children from the realities of the Third Reich for as long as they could. In 1935, they and the children were stripped of their citizenship. In May 1938, they fled Berlin with little more than the clothes on their backs. Before they left Berlin, Else mailed a box of loose gems and twelve gold snuff boxes to the friends they were going to stay with in The Hague. Miraculously, the parcel made it through German censors, providing the family with start-up funds for their new life.

When they were stopped trying to cross the border into Holland, Rifat used his stamp collection to bribe a German officer and gain their exit from Germany.

The Germans invaded Holland on May 10, 1940, after repeatedly assuring the Dutch they had no interest in occupying their country. Rifat immediately stepped up his plans to flee again. He arranged passage for the family with the captain of a fishing boat, who lost his courage when the moment came to sail to England the afternoon Rotterdam was bombed. Rifat ordered him, at gunpoint, to take them, an act that undoubtedly saved all their lives. By this time, Rifat's name was in Hitler's notorious Black Book, his "special arrest list" that had been drawn up in the event of a successful invasion of Great Britain. That, thankfully, never took place. As predicted by Meneer Visser, many Dutch, outraged by the invasion of their country and the treatment of Dutch Jews, mounted a fierce resistance to the Nazis. But, by the end of the war, the Jewish population of Holland was just a quarter of what it had been when the war began.

The Avigdor family made it across the North Sea, arriving in Folkestone on May 16, 1940. They stayed for a few days at The Grand Hotel, which was used as a base of operations for British pilots prior to, and during, the Battle of Britain. I have extended their stay in Folkestone for dramatic purposes. While there are no longer any records, older citizens of Folkestone remember Winston Churchill being at the hotel on several occasions, travelling there quietly, in stark contrast to Adolf Hitler, who was nearly always accompanied by a large retinue. On May 17, 1942, The Grand was shelled. The pilots staying there were saved because they were on church parade at the time. Again, for dramatic purposes, I have moved that incident forward two years. Four spies from the Netherlands were captured by military patrols when they landed on the Kent coast, south of Folkestone, in May 1940. Three of them were executed; the fourth was acquitted. Their story was made public in May 2007 when secret files from the National Archives were released.

Käfer, Mama, Bibi, and Peter sailed to Canada on the *SS Warwick Castle*. Rifat went separately on the *SS Nerissa*. Both ships made it safely to Canada, but those were dangerous times to be travelling the Atlantic. Before the end of the war, both the *Warwick Castle* and the *Nerissa* were torpedoed by U-boats and sunk. All told, 300 passengers and crew were drowned; 457 survived.

Once in Toronto, Canada, Rifat established an aeronautical parts company, continued to patent aeroplane parts, and rebuilt a substantial portion of his wealth in just eight years before dying in February 1949. He and Else never discussed their Jewish heritage with their children, and Käfer didn't know for certain that he was a Jew until he was 50 years old.

Käfer became a successful television director and producer. Ellen was a painter and Peter, an industrial designer.

Aunt Charlotte was murdered in a concentration camp during the war.

Acknowledgements

Writing is a solitary pursuit, but it takes a small army of people to bring a novel to publication, and I am blessed that so many people generously contributed their time and talent to *Boy from Berlin*.

Thanks to my goddaughter, Trilby Kent, herself an award-winning young adult novelist, who took time away from her own writing, teaching, and young daughter to assure me that I could write this book—and who then did the first edit.

To Antonia Banyard, editor extraordinaire, who pushed me to delve deeper into the characters and the story and, in the process, helped me take the book to a whole new level.

And, to Mary Ann Blair, my publisher, who sent me an email on a Sunday evening to say, "I'm partway through the book and I really, really like it. I decided after the first chapter that I definitely want to work with you on this." And who has been endlessly supportive throughout.

Käfer was a young boy when his family began their flight from Hitler's Europe. His memories are closely intertwined with those of so many young people who lived through World War II in Germany and Holland. Some later wrote about their experiences, which helped to inform *Boy from Berlin*, and I am very grateful to them.

And, finally, thank you to my friends and family for their unwavering encouragement and interest in getting Käfer's story told and to everyone who reads *Boy from Berlin*. I hope you enjoyed Käfer's story and will take a moment to post a review and recommend it to your friends. Käfer's adventures have just begun, so watch for the sequel!

About the Author

Nancy McDonald's career as a journalist included the television programs *W5, Canada AM,* and *Marketplace;* she then went on to become a sought-after freelance writer, penning everything from documentaries to live-action scripts to comic books.

Boy from Berlin is her first full-length novel. She's working on a sequel.

Nancy lives in Stratford, Ontario, where she revels in Shakespeare, takes theatregoers on tours of the Costume Warehouse, and treads the boards with the Perth County Players.

She invites you to visit her at **www.nancymcdonald.ca**.

CPSIA information can be obtained
at www.ICGtesting.com
Printed in the USA
LVHW092132141118
597187LV00001B/40/P